Life was better in Business Class, especially when your cheating ex-husband was paying for it. Hallelujah couldn't wait until Lloyd got the bill—for the airline ticket, the set of top-of-the-line TUMI luggage, the fashionable, Italian-worthy wardrobe, a two-week stay at a first-class hotel in Florence, an expensive day of pampering at the hotel spa, dinner in the city's finest restaurant, and front row seats to the Il Volo concert. It's not like Lloyd Evans couldn't afford it. It would hardly make a dent in the bastard's bank account.

Her short-term plan was to spend as much of Lloyd's money as she could before his skanky secretary/fiancée Olivia Brewster got her greedy little hands on it. *Polly would be proud of me.*

But she wasn't Polly. Polly lived life on the wild side, and she had a vindictive streak. Hallie Evans was practical. She believed in playing it safe and paying her own way. But she deserved this final fling. She had scraped together the last of her savings, and she would use those funds when Lloyd's credit card was tapped out. Then she would go back to the single life and the single paycheck and try not to dwell on how much her ex had hurt and humiliated her. But right now, Polly was in the pilot's seat. And, from now on, Hallie was determined to live life on the edge, just like Polly.

Settling into her roomy *Magnifica* seat, she signaled the Alitalia flight attendant for another amaretto sour before the plane took off. Getting properly sloshed mid-air was a strategic and recent addendum to the plan. Oh, and part of her plan was to swear off men.

Praise for Marilyn Baron and...

STUMBLE STONES

"Modern characters find themselves thrown into a mystery that spans generations, and to discover the answers, they have to look to the past. Marilyn Baron perfectly blends that laugh-out-loud humor of a new romance with the heartbreaking story of a family torn apart by the Holocaust. Touching and beautifully written with marvelous attention to setting and history."

~*Jennifer Moore, Author of Change of Heart*

"Marilyn Baron brings a unique style to her quirky and fast-paced stories that keeps readers turning pages."

~*New York Times Bestseller Dianna Love*

UNDER THE MOON GATE

"A surefire blockbuster... a treasure trove of mystery and intrigue. It sparkles with romance." ~*Andrew Kirby*

"Historical romance at its best." ~*TripFiction*

"A great job of bringing Bermuda during the WWII era to life." ~*PJ Ausdenmore, The Romance Dish*

"An enjoyable read from start to finish...family, friends, enemies, intrigue and suspense."

~*Romance Junkies (4 Blue Ribbons)*

LANDLOCKED

"*LANDLOCKED* is a well-researched, well-written story... A solid and fun book. Well worth the read!"

~*Veronica, Coffee Time Romance & More (4 Cups)*

"Baron offers a bit of everything.... There's humor, infidelity, murder, mayhem, and a neatly drawn conclusion."

~*RT Book Reviews (4.5 Stars)*

Stumble Stones
A Novel

by

Marilyn Baron

This is a work of fiction. Names, characters, places, and incidents are either the product of the author's imagination or are used fictitiously, and any resemblance to actual persons living or dead, business establishments, events, or locales, is entirely coincidental.

Stumble Stones
A Novel

COPYRIGHT © 2016 by Marilyn Baron

All rights reserved. No part of this book may be used or reproduced in any manner whatsoever without written permission of the author or The Wild Rose Press, Inc., except in the case of brief quotations embodied in critical articles or reviews.
Contact Information: info@thewildrosepress.com

Cover Art by *Debbie Taylor*

The Wild Rose Press, Inc.
PO Box 708
Adams Basin, NY 14410-0708
Visit us at www.thewildrosepress.com

Publishing History
First Crimson Rose Edition, 2016
Print ISBN 978-1-5092-0911-8
Digital ISBN 978-1-5092-0912-5

Published in the United States of America

Dedication

This book is dedicated to my husband, Steve,
who prefers to read spy thrillers set in World War II,
in hopes that he'll read this one.
Also to my two daughters, Marissa and Amanda,
who are my biggest cheerleaders,
and my new son-in-law, Adam Kallin.

Acknowledgments

Thanks to my friend Karl Goetzke for his e-mail about the stumble stones placed in front of his house in Stuttgart, Germany, which sparked the idea for this book. Stumble Stones is a real project. German artist Gunter Demnig has placed five thousand of these brass plaques—known as *Stolpersteine* or "stumble stones," cobblestone-sized Holocaust memorial stones—in Berlin and some fifty thousand of them in eighteen countries in Europe.

And a special thanks to my friend, *New York Times* Bestseller Dianna Love, my first reader and brainstormer extraordinaire, for her advice and support.

PART 1

AS THE PLANET SPINS

Marilyn Baron

Chapter One
Hallelujah

AS THE PLANET SPINS SCRIPT EXTRACT
BY HALLELUJAH WEISS
SCENE 1. THE KITCHEN AT THE WINTHROP ESTATE.
[PARKER AND POLLY IN KITCHEN. PARKER TOSSES HIS SUIT JACKET OVER A KITCHEN CHAIR, NOTICES POLLY, AND FROWNS.]
PARKER: [BLINKING] I'm beat, Polly. Can we talk tomorrow?
POLLY: [RAISES HER EYEBROWS] Hard night at the office?
PARKER: You have no idea.
POLLY: [SWEETLY] Oh, I think I do. Was your secretary there with you?
PARKER: I told you she would be. I asked her to work overtime.
POLLY: [CRYPTICALLY] What else did you ask her to do?
PARKER: [TURNS TOWARD POLLY] What are you implying?
POLLY: I'm not implying anything. As a matter of fact, I went to the office this evening to bring you your briefcase. You left it on the kitchen table.
PARKER: [FIDGETS WITH HIS TIE AS THE MUSIC INTENSIFIES; COUGHS TO CLEAR HIS THROAT]

You were at the office tonight?
POLLY: Imagine my surprise when I found the lights off and no one was there. I called your cell, but there was no answer. I left you a number of messages.
PARKER: Well, after we finished our project, we decided to get a bite to eat.
POLLY: Hmm. How long have I known you, Parker?
PARKER: A long time.
POLLY: Long enough to know when you're lying to me. Just tell me where you really were.
PARKER: You won't believe me anyway.
POLLY: This isn't the first time you've cheated on me.
PARKER: Polly, my secretary doesn't mean a thing to me. You're the love of my life. How many times have I married you?
POLLY: Too many to count.
PARKER: It's three, and I'd marry you all over again.
POLLY: It's too late for us, Parker.
PARKER: Let's take a trip. How would you like to go to Italy? Tuscany is beautiful this time of year.
POLLY: If I want to go to Italy, I'll go myself.
PARKER: You're so predictable.
POLLY: Not anymore. [GRABS PARKER BY THE LAPELS AND PLANTS A LONG, WET KISS ON HIS LIPS]
PARKER: What was that for?
POLLY: [ABRUPTLY] That, my dear husband, is called a kiss-off. Her smell is all over you. Go wash it off and pack your things. I want you gone before I wake up—and, oh, by the way, I want a divorce.

****

Life was better in Business Class, especially when your cheating ex-husband was paying for it. Hallelujah couldn't wait until Lloyd got the bill—for the airline ticket, the set of top-of-the-line TUMI luggage, the fashionable, Italian-worthy wardrobe, a two-week stay at a first-class hotel in Florence, an expensive day of pampering at the hotel spa, dinner in the city's finest restaurant, and front row seats to the Il Volo concert. It's not like Lloyd Evans couldn't afford it. It would hardly make a dent in the bastard's bank account.

Her short-term plan was to spend as much of Lloyd's money as she could before his skanky secretary/fiancée Olivia Brewster got her greedy little hands on it. *Polly would be proud of me.*

But she wasn't Polly. Polly lived life on the wild side, and she had a vindictive streak. Hallie Evans was practical. She believed in playing it safe and paying her own way. But she deserved this final fling. She had scraped together the last of her savings, and she would use those funds when Lloyd's credit card was tapped out. Then she would go back to the single life and the single paycheck and try not to dwell on how much her ex had hurt and humiliated her. But right now, Polly was in the pilot's seat. And, from now on, Hallie was determined to live life on the edge, just like Polly.

Settling into her roomy *Magnifica* seat, she signaled the Alitalia flight attendant for another amaretto sour before the plane took off. Getting properly sloshed mid-air was a strategic and recent addendum to the plan. Oh, and part of her plan was to swear off men.

Now that she was free and clear of Mr. Wrong, her long-term plan was to reinvent herself and revert back to her maiden name—Hallelujah Weiss. Lloyd was so cavalier he couldn't be bothered to use her birth name;

he had insisted on shortening her given name, Hallelujah, which she thought was distinctive, to Hallie. Like she wasn't worth the effort. So naturally, while Parker was conducting his affair with his secretary, he had stopped calling his wife Pollyanna and shortened it to Polly.

Hallelujah was expecting a nice settlement from her ex, but who knows what terms the lawyers would finally hammer out. She was convinced he'd hidden his assets, so her lawyer had hired an accountant to get to the bottom of that particular barrel, but she didn't expect to get a fraction of what was coming to her. Already Lloyd had gotten custody of their condo, and she had nowhere to live at the moment.

She'd always fantasized about living in Italy. She could write soap opera scripts from anywhere in the world. Have laptop—will travel. She'd taken two weeks off from her job as a writer for *As the Planet Spins* to get herself together, so she was free and clear to go wherever she wanted. When would she ever get a chance like this again? Her life was a blank slate—perfect for making a clean break. She didn't relish living on the same continent as Lloyd and Livia. Cutler's Ridge, California, was a small community, and she couldn't face running into the newly happy couple every time she went to the grocery store to binge on gelato to drown her sorrows.

When she told her best friend about her decision, RaeLynn had asked, "Isn't Italy a little drastic?"

"Desperate times…you get the picture."

And speaking of pictures, when she and RaeLynn were clearing her things out of the condo before Lloyd and Livia returned from Paris, she accidentally helped herself to the Monet painting. Maybe running off with the Monet was a little over the top, but Lloyd had run off with Olivia, hadn't he? Was taking the Monet legal? Probably not. Was cheating on her with his secretary legal? Who knew? Who cared? It certainly was immoral. Morality aside, the Monet was rightfully hers. Lloyd had purchased the small oil painting on canvas for her in a gallery near their hotel on their honeymoon. He wouldn't know a masterpiece if it bit him in the butt. He didn't appreciate fine art, and he didn't appreciate her.

Then RaeLynn admitted she'd never really liked Lloyd but hadn't said anything because she didn't want to ruin Hallelujah's happiness.

"Lloyd already took care of that."

When RaeLynn was rooting around in Lloyd's side of the closet, she unearthed a cardboard box. "Hey, this looks promising. What's in here?"

"Oh, just a box of Lloyd's deflated balls."

"What?"

"Some of his old tennis balls."

Hallelujah decided to dump Lloyd's balls and store the Monet in the box before removing it from the premises.

She'd left behind the ugly palm tree lamp Lloyd hated, pulling the plug on the lamp and her former life while she wrapped the brown cord around the monstrosity's neck, pretending the neck belonged to her former husband.

The lamp was tacky and kitschy. She was sophisticated, open to new possibilities. Like Pollyanna Winthrop, or Polly, the soap opera character she wrote for the long-running sudser *As the Planet Spins.*

Speaking of Pollyanna, the absurdly perky flight attendant was back with another sweet-smelling, mind-numbing cocktail. She couldn't wait until this flight got off the ground. Flying was not one of her favorite things.

"*Grazie*," said Hallelujah, slurring her Rs. She stored her Italian language book in the seat pocket in front of her, downed her second cocktail, and watched the flight attendant scurry off to fluff another passenger's pillow before filling her drink order. This was a record for her, and it didn't include the countless drinks she'd already put away on the transatlantic flight from California to Berlin. Only one leg of the trip to go and she'd be in Italy—her happy place.

She made a decent living as a soap opera writer, but every time she told someone what she did, they would snicker as if it weren't a respectable profession. She had studied creative writing in college and wanted to become a serious writer, perhaps write a novel. But she needed a high-concept idea. She hoped she would find one on this trip to Italy. Now that she was on her own, she didn't think it was wise to quit her day job.

A tall, lanky, well-dressed man in a neat goatee took the seat next to her. A tall, lanky, *attractive* man. Hallelujah studied the hottie surreptitiously, her gaze traversing his face. Moving past the thick black glasses framing enigmatic, steel-gray eyes, she was stopped in her tracks by the facial hair. Normally she wasn't attracted to men with beards, but life after divorce was anything but normal. This man had possibilities, *if* he'd shave his beard. Was it too early into their relationship to suggest it? Probably. *What would Polly do?* She knew what Polly would do. Polly would have this man eating out of her hands before the plane reached cruising altitude.

He'd only been in his seat five minutes, and they hadn't even been properly introduced. Hallelujah felt a little high—would soon feel at least 35,000 feet high—and far away from the constraints of California, which made her feel naughty, and that felt great. Her plan to swear off men now seemed seriously shortsighted.

He turned to face her. His goatee was starting to slip. Either that or she'd had too much to drink.

"Hi, I'm Lucca. Thought I'd introduce myself, since we're going to be seatmates for the next hour and fifty-eight minutes, until we land in Rome."

It probably couldn't hurt to talk to him. She shook his hand. "I'm Hallelujah Weiss."

He smiled, and when he did, he took his dimples for a test flight. "Hallelujah as in 'Hallelujah, brother'?"

"No, Hallelujah, as in that's the name my parents gave me when I was born." She was a rabbi's daughter. She might as well own it. Even though her father trivialized her profession and said writing for soap operas "promulgated the propaganda of seduction." Her parents claimed they never watched the show, but Hallelujah happened to know that, although she'd never admit it, her mother was a closet fan of the soap.

"No nicknames? Hal? Louie?"

"No, just plain Hallelujah."

The man studied her appreciatively. "From where I sit, there's nothing plain about you."

"Well, then you'd better change seats or get new glasses. Not everyone in the world thinks so."

"Hallelujah is quite a mouthful for such a tiny girl," he noted.

She loved that he thought she was tiny. She always felt ungainly next to Lloyd's petite secretary/lover. Even seated, Lucca was so tall anyone would look small in comparison.

Lucca also had a very sexy Italian accent to go with his very sexy body (as she imagined it, sans beard). Hallelujah focused on the man's mouth. It would be entirely kissable if that damn goatee weren't covering it. The beard would have to go if he had any intention of kissing her, Hallelujah speculated.

"What brings you to Rome?" Hallelujah asked, wanting to be sociable.

"A broken heart."

Hallelujah sat up in her seat. "Someone dumped you, too?"

The hottie looked down at his newspaper. "I'd rather not discuss it. It's personal."

"You can talk to me. I'm a good listener. And I'll bet my story could top yours."

With a look of resignation, Lucca turned to her. "It's a classic. Sigrid and I…Sigrid *was* my fiancée, and we were ready to walk down the aisle. She was pregnant, and I was having the house remodeled to please her and accommodate the baby."

"Then what happened?" Hallelujah asked, thinking this had the makings of a great story.

"Her ex-husband happened. Turns out he was the father of the baby—she'd been sleeping with him for months behind my back. We were about to take a Scandinavian cruise for our honeymoon. I still have the tickets. Non-refundable."

"That's horrible," Hallelujah agreed. "What are you going to do?"

"I'm going to take care of some business in Rome and then go on the cruise without her."

"What kind of business?"

"You ask a lot of questions for a woman I just met."

"I'm naturally curious."

"Okay. I'm giving a speech at an economics conference."

"What are you going to talk about?"

"I doubt you'd find it interesting."

"Try me."

"It's about fiscal policy reform and stimulus, how to survive volatile markets, and how low and negative interest rates in some countries are holding down the economy and fueling a looming retirement crisis. I'll also be addressing the viability of the EU."

Hallelujah snorted. "You're right. That's a mouthful. Exactly what kind of work do you do?"

"I'm a hedge fund manager in Berlin."

"I've never been to Berlin, and I have no interest in going there."

"Why not?"

"Well, for one thing, I'm Jewish, and for another, my father is a rabbi."

"Berlin is actually a very interesting place."

"If you say so. Are you any good at what you do?"

"I work for the number one firm in Europe, and we're performing well in a challenging market environment. But enough about me. What about you? What brings you to Rome?"

Hallelujah frowned and shrugged. "I'm the other side of the same coin. A woman scorned. I found out my husband and his secretary had been cheating on me for more than a year. I can't say I didn't see it coming. All the classic signs were there. The late nights, the sudden business trips, the telephone hang-ups. He wasn't sleeping with me, so I knew he must be sleeping with someone else. But did I do anything about it? No. How stupid am I? It wasn't until I walked in on them one night in his office and they were naked on his couch. It was staring me right in the face then, so I could no longer deny it." *I should have attacked the situation head-on, which is how Polly would have handled things.*

"I'm thinking of selling the house," Lucca said. "I don't need such a big place. I love that house, but—"

"I can top that. I don't even have a house to go back to."

Lucca rubbed his chin and fidgeted in his seat, then pulled out a package from his briefcase.

Another nervous flyer. She wasn't the only one.

"Say, um, Hallelujah with no nicknames, I need to use the restroom. Would you hold on to this package for me until I get back? It's a gift for my mother, and it's fragile. I don't want to take a chance it will break if we encounter any turbulence."

Hallelujah narrowed her eyes. She might have been well on the way to being wasted, but wasn't there some rule about accepting suspicious packages from strangers? No, that was inside the airport, and this man had obviously cleared security, so whatever was in this package was safe. The old Hallie would have turned him down. The new, free-spirited, adventurous Hallelujah had nothing to lose. She nodded. Why not? They were seatmates, after all.

Lucca handed her the package and headed toward

the back of the plane.

"Hey, I think you're going the wrong way. The Business Class restrooms are in the front. And we're about to take off. You have to be in your seat." Spoken like a true schoolmarm or a fussy librarian. A real rule follower. Who did she think she was, a flight attendant? But he was already gone.

Hallelujah ran her fingers around the package and squeezed. It was compact but substantial, and whatever was inside felt like marbles or stones. It didn't feel fragile or breakable. Her natural curiosity took hold. Her mother always told her curiosity killed the cat, but when had she ever listened to her mother? She'd married Lloyd against her mother's advice, hadn't she? Her mother had warned her that Lloyd was too handsome for his own good. But Hallelujah was a writer, and writers, like cats, were naturally curious creatures.

Would she have time to sneak a peek at the package before the stranger returned? If the package was so valuable, then why didn't he take it with him? Why was she even hesitating? She was dying to find out what was in the package. It might tell her a little about the man who possessed it. And right now, he had her at a disadvantage. She knew almost nothing about him, except that he'd been jilted.

Gingerly, she unwrapped the gift. Inside the wrapping was a black velvet bag with a drawstring. How hard would it be to steal a glance to find out what the hottie had been hiding?

Hallelujah frowned. He'd been gone quite a long time, long enough to go to the bathroom ten times over, unless he was airsick. She looked at her watch. The plane was already in the air and thirty minutes had passed since she'd seen him. The seatbelt sign was off, and she had permission to move about the cabin, but instead she pressed her call button to summon the flight attendant, who came immediately. Hallelujah carefully stashed the package in her purse.

"Excuse me. I mean, *scusi*. But the gentleman who was sitting next to me, he was tall with a goatee and black glasses? He left to go to the restroom, and he never came back. He wasn't in his seat for takeoff. I don't know what could have happened. Could you please check on him? I think there must be something wrong."

The flight attendant excused herself, disappeared behind the curtain, and returned promptly. "I'm sorry, miss, but I reviewed the passenger manifest and, just as I thought, the seat next to you is empty."

Hallelujah took a deep breath. "I can see that it's empty *now*, but it wasn't empty almost an hour ago. There was a man sitting next to me. He said his name was Lucca. I don't think he gave his last name. Probably something Italian, but he was definitely here." Maybe he had given her a false name.

The flight attendant rolled her eyes and took Hallelujah's two empty glasses. "Perhaps you'd like another amaretto sour?"

"I'm not drunk," Hallelujah insisted, drumming her fingers impatiently on the seat tray. "I know what I saw. There was a man in the seat next to me, and he seems to have disappeared. He can't be too difficult to find. He was very—distinctive-looking. He was Italian, or at least he had an Italian accent."

The flight attendant perfected her eye roll. "Now,

what are the chances a man with an Italian accent would be on an Alitalia flight from Berlin to Rome?" When Hallelujah frowned, she added, "I'll do a quick check in coach and search the lavatories to see what I can find."

"Yes, please do that." Whatever happened to the concept of customer service? Wasn't the passenger always right?

Hallelujah stuck her hand in her purse and rubbed the hidden bag, half expecting a genie to appear. She should probably turn the package over to the flight crew, but not until she determined what was in it.

When the flight attendant returned, she shook her head. "There's no one on this flight resembling the man you described."

"That's impossible," Hallelujah insisted. "Maybe you should look again."

"And as I said, there is no one assigned to the seat next to you."

"Well, maybe he came up from coach and just sat here before takeoff."

The flight attendant shrugged. "That wouldn't be the first time."

"Yes, that must be what happened."

"Is there anything else I can get you?"

Hallelujah shook her head, and the flight attendant turned to walk away.

She picked up her purse and felt for the package. Okay, she was going to find out what was in it. If it was so valuable, then he'd be back for it. What if it was a bomb? What if the man were a terrorist? Highly likely in this day and age, given all the recent incidents in Europe. But it didn't feel like a bomb. And Lucca hadn't sounded like a terrorist. She was exhausting herself jumping to all these conclusions.

The package was too soft to be a bomb. It wasn't ticking, and it hadn't exploded—yet. Lloyd always said she was predictable. Well, the old Hallie would have left well enough alone. The new Hallelujah, however, was about to enter uncharted territory. She stuck her hand into the bag again, praying it didn't get blown off, and pulled the drawstring loose. Then she looked inside.

Hallelujah's eyes bulged as she inhaled a liqueur-scented breath. The bag was filled with dazzling diamonds of all shapes, sizes, and colors. They were brilliantly cut and glimmering, even in the low light of the cabin. There must be millions of dollars of diamonds in her purse. The man would definitely be coming back for them. Unless someone had killed him onboard or he had gotten off the plane at the last minute, before it took off, which was possible. Or maybe she had watched one too many thriller movies on the international flight to Europe. Because when she last saw him, he had been headed toward the rear of the aircraft, so leaving the plane was unlikely.

Her imagination was running away with her. Should she report the incident? No. The flight attendant was already convinced she was hallucinating or drunk. She *was* drunk. On Disaronno and diamonds.

For all she knew, he could be an international jewel thief—a cat burglar. Ha, ha. Maybe he was a James Bond-type British agent, disguised as a hunky Italian businessman.

She closed the drawstring and zipped the package securely into the deep pocket of her oversized purse.

She held her breath and patted the beads of perspiration on her forehead with the white paper drink napkin as the weight of the world came crashing down around her shoulders. She didn't want to be responsible for all of these diamonds. She should probably turn them over to the flight attendant. But what if Lucca came back? The sooner they landed in Rome, the better.

First, she was going to search the plane and find the man who claimed to be Lucca. He couldn't have disappeared into thin air. He wasn't Houdini, for Pete's sake. He didn't have a parachute, that she knew of. She got up from her seat, securely clutching her purse against her body. Did she look suspicious? Her feverish brow surely telegraphed nerves. Hopefully, there wasn't an air marshal on the flight. Swaying down the aisle, she balanced against the seatbacks as she moved, looking from left to right, almost tripping over the foot of one clumsy passenger, until she had covered the entire length of the plane. Unless he was in the restroom, Italian Hottie Mystery Man was not onboard.

Wait a minute. That guy in the window seat looked familiar. She stared at the scrumptious-looking Italian, his face partially hidden behind a copy of *Corriere della Sera*. Only he was holding the newspaper upside down, which either spoke to his versatility and his ability to read Italian upside down or indicated he couldn't read Italian at all, which meant he wasn't really Italian, as he had claimed to be. He didn't have a goatee, and he wasn't wearing glasses. It wasn't her guy. Other passengers were beginning to regard her suspiciously. It was time to get back to the business-class cabin.

Firmly settled back in her seat, she finally felt safe.

She couldn't sleep. She had to keep her wits about her. The man had obviously just pulled off a major heist. And she was as good as his accomplice. What should she do with the diamonds? Would there be bomb-sniffing dogs at the airport when she stepped off the plane? *Carabinieri* with machine guns? Would they be looking for her? She didn't fancy being interrogated or spending time in an Italian prison—or any prison, for that matter. What would she do when she got to Rome? *What would Polly do?*

Chapter Two

AS THE PLANET SPINS SCRIPT EXTRACT
BY HALLELUJAH WEISS
SCENE 2. IN THE MASTER BEDROOM AT THE WINTHROP ESTATE.

POLLY: [ACCEPTS A PACKAGE FROM PARKER] What's this?
PARKER: Why don't you open it and find out?
POLLY: I don't want anything from you.
PARKER: They say good things come in small packages.
POLLY: [LOOKS DOWN AT PARKER'S SLACKS AND CHOKES WITH LAUGHTER] Well, apparently they haven't seen your package.
PARKER: I'm serious, Polly. I've missed you. I said I was sorry. It will never happen again. I hope this gift makes up for it.
POLLY: [OPENS THE JEWELRY BOX] You can't buy me off with a piece of—Is this an engagement ring?
PARKER: What do you say we make it an even four?
POLLY: I'll say one thing, Parker, you have good taste in jewelry. (SHE TRIES ON THE FLASHY DIAMOND ENGAGEMENT RING.)
PARKER: You like the ring?
POLLY: I love the ring; it's you I'm not so sure about. You're too handsome for your own good.

PARKER: Is that a Yes?
POLLY: It's a Maybe. But either way, I'm keeping the ring. You owe me that much.

****

Hallelujah didn't have long to wait.

As soon as she deplaned and retrieved her luggage, a stranger grabbed her by the elbow, spun her around, and pulled her into his arms. He embraced her like he hadn't seen her in months. Like he hadn't seen a woman in years. Like he hadn't just seen her on the flight to Rome.

"Darling," he sighed convincingly—indeed, so convincingly she could feel his erection against her stomach. And that sexy voice. She'd know it anywhere. Apparently, Italians were very demonstrative.

"What are you doing here?" Hallelujah demanded, trying her best to recover. "What happened to your glasses? And your accent? And your goatee? Are you even a hedge fund manager?"

"Yes. I'll take that package now."

"Where did you get all those—"

Lucca clamped a hand over her mouth. "Don't say another word."

Hallelujah struggled to break free of his hold.

"So you looked in the package. You're a naughty girl, Hallelujah."

Hallelujah tried but failed to look innocent, and she knew it. Lloyd had always said she was an open book, that she'd make a poor poker player. She lifted her chin. "What if I did?"

"Then I'd have to kill you," the man said simply, in a tone that conveyed the idea that he meant it. She was still banded by his arms.

Hallelujah's eyes widened. "I hope you're joking. I came to Italy to get away from all the drama in my life. I don't need any attitude from you. Who are you, really?"

"Just give me the package, and I'll be on my way."

Hallelujah clutched her purse tightly. "Not until you tell me where you got these. Did you steal them?"

Lucca shook his head. "You're going to regret sticking your nose in where it doesn't belong."

"I already do. Now get your hands off me, or I'll call the police."

"You don't want to do that."

Out of the corner of her eye, Hallelujah glimpsed a stocky man with a gun moving toward them.

"That man has a gun," Hallelujah said hoarsely. She wanted to scream, but she couldn't get a sound out.

As the man got closer, Lucca pivoted to shield her with his body and turned them in the opposite direction.

"We've got to get out of here, now," Lucca ordered. "He won't shoot in a crowded airport."

Lucca released Hallelujah, lifted the handle of his suitcase, and rolled it out to trip the man approaching them. Then he reached down to the ground where the man lay, and pocketed the gun.

"Run, Hallelujah."

Hallelujah clutched her suitcase and purse and turned to Lucca, frozen in place. "What about the package?"

"Just give it to me. I'm sorry I got you involved in this." Another man approached, and Lucca signaled him and tossed him the weapon. "Silvio, please take my luggage to your condo. I'll meet you there. And for God's sake, do something with this gun."

People raced by with luggage, and the moving crowd shielded them from danger temporarily. No one seemed to notice the downed man now starting to get up. They pushed forward, eager to be on their way. Hallelujah didn't spot a single policeman in the area. Not even a guard dog. Soon she lost sight of the man.

"Now they've seen you with me," Lucca said. "Your life may be in danger."

"Who's *they*?"

Alexander hesitated. "That's just it. I don't know. I do know they want something I have. They must be after the diamonds. Someone broke into my house last night, after I had the diamonds appraised, and ransacked it. And they've been following me ever since I left Berlin. That's why I was in a disguise on the airplane. Someone already took a shot at me." Alexander met Hallelujah's eyes. "Will you be okay?"

Hallelujah's hands shook so she could hardly grip her suitcase handle.

"You're terrified."

"Don't leave me, please," she pleaded.

"You don't want to be mixed up in this. Give me the package and walk away."

Hallelujah stood rooted to the spot, still jostled by the crowd.

"Shit," Lucca cursed. "Okay," he said, striving for calm. "We're going to have to lose whoever is chasing us. Silvio, take her suitcases. Hallelujah, follow me."

"B-but I have a driver waiting to take me to Florence. And I don't even know you. Why should I go with you?"

"You shouldn't. But I can't leave you here alone. We don't have a choice now, Hallelujah, if that's even your real name."

"It is. I have dinner reservations at *Il Palagio* at the Four Seasons Hotel *Firenze*. And I have tickets to the Il Volo concert at the end of my stay. I can't miss that."

"The Ebola concert?"

"No. Il Volo."

"Who's Il Volo?"

"Are you kidding me?"

"No, but, whoever they are, fun will have to wait until we take care of business." He grabbed her arm again and clasped her roughly to his side, dragging her away from baggage claim.

Hallelujah pleaded, "L-let's just call the *Carabinieri*."

"I don't think you want to involve the police. You're the one with the diamonds. How will you explain them? I don't know who we can trust."

"How do I know I can trust you?"

"That's a chance you'll have to take."

"I highly doubt your name is even Lucca. Who are you really?"

The man calling himself Lucca rubbed his chin and frowned. "My name is Alexander Stone."

"Are you even Italian?"

"No," he admitted.

"That may be the first honest thing you've said to me, but I'm not going anywhere with you unless you tell me what this is all about."

"It's a long story. And we're out of time." He tugged on her shoulder. "You need to come with me, now," he declared emphatically.

"Or what?"

"It may already be too late." Alexander put his arm

around Hallelujah's shoulders and steered her toward the nearest exit.

She stopped in her tracks and turned to Alexander. "What about my bags? I can't just leave them here. My whole life is in these bags," she protested. "Or what's left of it. And my computer is in my carry-on. I can't go anywhere without it." Her computer was her connection with the world.

Alexander lifted her carry-on. "We'll take the carry-on, but my friend Silvio will bring our luggage to his condo. Then, if we're not followed, you can just go on your way."

The man Alexander called Silvio started loading their luggage onto a cart.

"Those are my bags!" she shouted. "Be careful with them."

"Keep your voice down, Hallelujah," Alexander ordered. "If you ever want to see your luggage again, you'll come with me." He tightened his grip on her arm.

Hallelujah asked herself, "What would Polly do?" *Go for it!* That's what Polly would do. Hallelujah was predictable. Polly was not. In fact, Polly was a bit reckless. Outside, horns honked and traffic whizzed by, and Hallelujah was nearly mowed down by a motorcycle.

"I can't believe I'm getting into a car with a complete stranger."

"Don't worry. You're not getting into a car. Have you ever ridden a motorcycle?"

Hallelujah's mouth hung open. "Motorcycles are dangerous." Parker had once taken a serious spill on a Harley. He'd been in a coma for months. It was touch-and-go there for a while. Polly had been nominated for a Daytime Emmy® for her portrayal of the distraught wife at his bedside. And then, soon after he recovered, Polly was kidnapped by a mysterious man on a motorcycle and they found her in an alley, beaten senseless. She remained in a coma for more than a year. Hallelujah had a bad feeling about motorcycles.

"Not if you know how to ride them." Alexander took her hand and walked up to a cherry-red Ducati. "Catch," he said, tossing her a helmet, after which he stored her carry-on in the motorcycle saddlebag.

"What do I do?" Hallelujah's voice rose an octave as Alexander fastened the helmet on her head.

"Just wrap your arms around my waist and don't let go. Lean into me on the turns. And close your eyes so you can't see the road. Italians are notoriously bad drivers."

"Is that how you ride, with your eyes closed?"

"Of course not."

"What if I can't do it?"

Alexander dismissed her. "It's just like sex. After you've done it once, it all comes back to you."

"Then I'm screwed," Hallelujah whispered, trying to remember the last time she and Lloyd had been together that way. In fact, last month, when she visited a fortune teller, the woman had grasped her palm and read, "I can see that your lotus flower is drying up because it's not being used." Was it that obvious?

"What did you say?" Alexander shouted, fastening his own helmet.

Hallelujah shook her head and mumbled, "Nothing. Where are we going?"

"For now, a condo owned by a business associate. We can't take any chances that they'll find us. I need to deliver my speech, but by tomorrow afternoon, we can be where no one will think to look."

"Where is that?" Hallelujah asked.

"On the high seas. You, Mrs. Stone, my lovely wife, and I, are going on a romantic Scandinavian cruise."

"What do you mean your *wife*?"

"I've already booked the cabin on a small ship, only nine hundred passengers, and it's our honeymoon cruise. So they upgraded us to the bridal suite. The travel agent assured me it was very private."

"I'm going on *your* honeymoon?"

"Yes, these people who are after me are looking for a single man, but now we'll be a couple. And no one will think to look for us in the middle of the North Sea."

"Why aren't you traveling under an assumed name?"

"The cruise line requires a passport number, so I have to use my real name."

"But you don't have *my* passport number."

Alexander rendered a sheepish smile and pulled her passport from his pocket.

"Where did you get that?" she demanded.

"I borrowed it from you on the plane. I'm going to hold on to it for safekeeping."

"I can't believe you *stole* my passport."

"Borrowed."

"You planned this from the beginning," Hallelujah accused. "You deliberately targeted me, planted the diamonds, and kidnapped me from the airport. I'm not sure I'm okay with this. You're a virtual stranger."

"Well, I suggest we use this evening to rectify that

and come to terms with each other."

"I hope you're not suggesting that we, that I—"

"I think it will be fun. It's been a while for me, and I'm overdue."

Hallelujah's mouth flew open. "You did not just say that."

Alexander smiled wickedly. "I meant it's been awhile since I've had any *fun*."

Hallelujah expelled a breath. "If I agree to this, there have to be some ground rules."

"And what might those be?"

"No hanky-panky."

"You're cute and very easy to tease."

"I mean it."

"Do you mean, no kissing?" Alexander, now straddling the motorcycle, steadied it with his feet on the ground as he turned around, maneuvered his arm around her shoulder, and kissed the breath out of her.

"I've been dying to do that since I saw you on the plane. And this…" He deliberately grazed the top of her breast with his hand and trailed his fingers further.

"Stop that." Hallelujah batted his hand away.

"Do you really want me to stop? If we're going to get away with this charade, we have to act like newlyweds."

The kiss had sent her reeling, and she wanted him never to stop, but if he knew that, he might think she was a horny slut. Sometimes, Polly was a horny slut. She had played musical beds with most of the eligible bachelors in the fictional town of Milano, even some of the married men, too, and evidently Polly was in the driver's seat. Or rather, Alexander Stone was in the driver's seat, and Hallelujah was just along for the ride.

Feeling the need to return to safer ground, she inquired, "What do you plan to do with the diamonds?"

"That's what I hope to figure out. The goal is to return them to their rightful owner, or at least the owner's family. The problem is I don't know who the owner is. The trail has gone cold. But we have plenty of time to do research on the ship until we disembark in Stockholm. That is, if you'll agree to come with me. I can't force you. But what do you have to lose? It's only a week, and it will be a first-class vacation for you."

"What about my reservations in Florence?"

"I'll cancel them," said Alexander, adding, "I'll tell you what. If this works out, and we're still alive at the end of the cruise, I'll treat you to a week at The Four Seasons in Florence."

"My ex-husband is already treating me to more than that, only he doesn't know it yet." After considering her situation, and wondering what Polly would do, Hallelujah relented. "I think you're either a very successful cat burglar or a con artist. But I'll agree to work with you. I'm unpredictable that way. This whole situation is unbelievable. It will make a great story."

Alexander turned around, moistened his lips, leaned back to kiss her again, and settled his body back against hers.

She narrowed her eyes.

"Just practicing," he said, before he tightened his helmet.

Barely able to draw a breath, Hallelujah latched on to Alexander, putting her body into it to show just how well she could play the game. They sped off toward the *autostrade*, past a vista of crumbling travertine stone, the ancient buildings giving off a glint of pale yellow in the morning sun. *Polly, I hope we don't live to regret this.*

Chapter Three
Alexander

Berlin/Dahlem, Germany

Alexander Stone had lived in Berlin for three years. It had been his choice to move there and accept the job with a German hedge fund so he could get back to his German roots, or rather, his parents' German roots. The city had a lot to offer. It was vibrant and alive, and spoke to his soul, with interesting cafés and bars and fine art galleries lining cobblestoned streets.

His German heritage pulsed in his blood, and through his soul, every time he walked around the city; whenever he viewed the fast-flowing River Spree or experienced the leafy tree-lined streets of the *Unter den Linden*, Berlin's premiere promenade and the tall trees in the *Tiergarten*, reforested after being plundered during the war by citizens desperate for firewood. He loved the history and beauty of the place, and its eclectic assortment of architecture, from the gentrified classical buildings to the modern structures that rose like a phoenix from the ashes of conflict, but he was too busy working to take advantage of it.

His love of the city hadn't translated to his personal life. He hadn't even met any eligible *Fräuleins*. When he passed the houses in his neighborhood, everyone seemed to have a place. Everyone seemed to be cozy and happy. Everyone had someone. Everyone belonged. Everyone except him.

None of his colleagues had offered to set him up on a date. They were too busy competing with each other. He'd wanted the whole Berlin experience, but so far, it had eluded him. He hadn't even had much time to travel around Europe, another elusive dream. He had given up his dream to further his career. And now he was rich and successful and, in his estimation, the loneliest man on the planet.

He discovered that dining by himself was even lonelier in a foreign country than it was in America. Passing by a restaurant, he caught himself looking longingly in the lighted window at all the happy couples. He imagined they were sharing their day, talking about mundane things, what happened at work, just enjoying a meal, enjoying being together. Or maybe they were planning a fabulous future or planning a family.

Then he had met Sigrid, and his life changed in a heartbeat. She was beautiful, intelligent, and she couldn't wait to have children. A real old-fashioned girl. His mother would love her. Her fondest wish was that he marry a German girl, but she was euphoric when Alexander announced his engagement to Sigrid, who was Scandinavian, and when Sigrid told him she was pregnant, he considered himself the happiest man in the world. He was starting life with his new family, and the world suddenly became brighter—until she finally admitted the truth: She was pregnant with her ex-husband's baby, and she was breaking their engagement and remarrying him.

He felt like he'd been flattened on the *U-Bahn*

tracks. He could hardly get out of bed in the morning. He'd stopped calling his mother because she prefaced all of her conversations with, "When am I going to see my new grandchild?" He didn't have the heart to tell her the wedding was off, and that in order to get a grandchild you first needed a wife. When he finally told her, she was devastated, but she said, "You just haven't found the right woman yet."

Then she added, "Do you expect your soulmate to fall out of the sky? You have to make an effort."

True, after Sigrid broke up with him, he hadn't made much of an effort to socialize with anyone. His feeling was that if something was meant to be, it would just happen. He might be a number cruncher, but along with his faith in numerical data, he did believe in destiny. And he was hopeful. He couldn't help but feel that something was coming. The world was open to possibilities.

In the meantime, he wasn't interested in dining alone, so most nights he stopped by *KaDeWe* on *Tauentzienstrasse* near the center of what used to be West Berlin, to pick up some prepared foods. The sixth and seventh floors were entirely devoted to gourmet food. With 40,000 to 50,000 visitors a day, the department store was usually mobbed, but somehow he felt less alone in a crowd, and every day he went home with a different dinner. With two football fields of food under one roof, that was easy to do.

Mostly, he walked with his head down, staring at the pavement, to and from the *U-Bahn* station, from which he was daily whisked to work in Berlin. Which is how he first discovered the *stolpersteine*, or "stumble stones," at the entranceway to the Bauhaus-style villa he had just bought in Dahlem, a southwestern borough of Berlin. Dahlem was one of the most affluent areas of the city, and his home, of which he was quite proud, was a white stucco exterior with three stories, nestled in an idyllic, quiet neighborhood.

The house was a stunner on the outside. It had everything. Everything, that is, but a family. And he was determined to change that. In fact, he had started renovation when Sigrid was still in his life and had almost finished a project he hoped would give the interior of the house a facelift and a nursery, which he now had no need for. He had initiated some changes, changes that might suit Sigrid, or the woman he would eventually share his life with, whoever she turned out to be. It was during the renovation project that workers had unearthed a metal box wedged in a secret compartment under the staircase; inside were the diamonds.

Alexander noticed the placard announcing a ceremony on the sidewalk in front of his multi-level mansion when he left for the office. He glanced at his watch. The ceremony was starting in a few minutes so, instead of being the first one into the office, as he usually was, he decided he needed to attend. Making a fortune for other people could wait.

It had started to snow lightly, the flakes kissing his cheek. He tightened the wool scarf around his neck and flexed his fingers to keep the blood flowing under the leather gloves. Despite the frozen precipitation, it was a glorious day. By this time of morning he would typically be in the office with his nose in front of a computer screen, sizing up world markets, oblivious to the weather outside. He lifted his head to the warmth of the sun and felt free, for the first time in a long time. The ceremony was starting. The placard promised music, poetry, and flowers. A man dressed in jeans and a leather jacket, with a broad-brimmed hat, was down on his knees on the pavement.

Alexander nudged an elderly gentleman next to him whom he recognized as his neighbor. He'd seen the man walking his dog every morning and waved, but they hadn't officially met. He'd toyed with the idea of getting a dog to keep him company, but it would have been selfish to leave a dog sitting home alone all day.

"Who is that man down on the ground?" Alexander asked.

"That is the German artist Gunter Demnig. He makes the *stolpersteine*, the stumble stones," the neighbor explained. "Handcrafts each one."

"What are *stolpersteine*?"

"They are small concrete blocks in the ground, covered by a brass plaque. They are mini memorials to the Jews, and other victims of the Holocaust—socialists, the so-called 'mentally defective,' the gypsies."

Alexander recalled reading something about the memorial monuments all over Berlin, placed on sidewalks in front of homes or apartment buildings. He'd experienced the proper amount of guilt, as a German-American, for the sins of the fathers, not his father in particular, but for the Nazis and the irreparable damage they did to decency during the war. But he had never seen one of these stones in person.

Alexander watched with fascination as the artist positioned and anchored each stone in the ground, flush with the sidewalk. Then the man covered each stone with a brass plaque.

"Every letter on every plaque is hand carved by the artist or one of his apprentices," noted his neighbor. "Every plaque contains a name, the year of birth, the date the victim was deported, and the place and date of death. We are lucky to have the artist himself here today."

Alexander got closer. "*Hier wohnte,*" he read.

"Here lived," translated the neighbor, assuming that Alexander was not fluent in German. "This was the last known home of the person or persons who lived in this house, the house where you're now living. There are four stones lined up together, representing the family who lived here. Sometimes they place the stones where the victim worked or studied. The artist has placed five thousand of them right here in Berlin and some fifty thousand of them in more than six hundred fifty German towns and cities and even in countries surrounding Germany. He's made it his life's work. He's no longer a young man, as you can see. He is very dedicated."

A crowd had gathered to watch the artist work as he mixed the concrete, formed each block, no higher than sidewalk level, and finally affixed the plaque on top of the stone, each letter stamped in the brass.

Alexander moved through the crowd to get a closer look and noticed the 4x4-inch plaques. He read the names silently. Julian, 1894; Ana, 1901; Hannah, 1928; and Aaron, 1942. And under each birth year: *Deportiert* Auschwitz 1943 and in Auschwitz *ermordet* (died) that same year.

According to his neighbor, someone had paid more than a hundred Euros to fashion each plaque and research the facts of the family's story.

"If you want to learn more about the people who are memorialized, you can access the project database," his neighbor added.

When the artist was finished, someone spoke. After the ceremony, music played and a group of schoolchildren sang, read poetry, and laid flowers by the stones. Imagine that: a little piece of the past come alive right in front of his house.

His neighbor came up behind him. "Not everyone approves of these stones. Sometimes they are smeared with tar during the night. But the artist comes back and removes it.

"Even Jewish leaders sometimes object that people walk all over the plaques. But it's not meant to desecrate. Its intention is to memorialize the victims and preserve their memories. You don't stumble *over* the plaques, because they are street level, but you stumble *upon* them."

"Are you—" Alexander began.

"If you are asking if I am a Jew, yes, I am. I'm a survivor. There aren't many of us left. I didn't know the family, but I feel as if I did."

Alexander was silent. He didn't know what he was supposed to say. He felt a little uncomfortable, guilty even, though he had nothing to feel guilty about. His boss and the founder of his company were Jewish. Some of his coworkers were. But he hadn't given it much thought. He decided that he liked the idea of the memorial in front of his house.

Alexander went up to the artist.

"Why are these stones at an angle to my house?"

"I place some markers at an angle to the building

and some straight and some on asphalt sidewalks and some on cobblestones because I want some variation both physically and artistically," the artist remarked. "So you live here, in the house where the Hirschfelds lived?"

Alexander nodded.

And suddenly it hit him. This family, the Hirschfelds—father, mother, daughter, and young son—once lived where he was now living. Before the war. Before they were seized by the Nazis and carried away on crowded trains to their deaths. He was the usurper, living in their house. None of the Hirschfelds appeared to have survived the war. Who had taken over their house after they were deported? Was that person still alive? Did the family have relatives who had survived? Were the survivors ever compensated for the house and property that was stolen from them? It was important that he find out. More important than work. More important than anything in his life right now. He was desperate to solve the mystery, so he decided to skip work and start his research.

There wasn't much to go on. The Germans were good record keepers, so he had no doubt he could find out the owner of the house after the war and the people who had lived there up until the time he had purchased it. Alexander was methodical. That's the way his mind worked. He was going to track down the facts. He owed it to the Hirschfelds. He longed to know more of their story. Fate had placed him in this house, in the house where these people had once lived, for a reason, and he was determined to find out what that reason was.

Marilyn Baron

PART TWO

A PORTRAIT OF EVIL
The SS Officer's Woman

Marilyn Baron

Chapter Four
Hannah

Berlin 1943

"Ready or not, here I come. I am coming to find you, *liebchen.*"

Hannah sat, shoulders scrunched, in her hiding place under the stairwell as her mother's voice got colder and colder. *Mutter* was probably carrying her baby brother, Aaron, who was being particularly fussy that morning, so she might have been confused and turned around. Aaron was too little to understand what was happening, but he knew something monumental was occurring, and he was making his displeasure known by fretting and demanding to be held. This time Hannah had chosen a very good hiding place where no one could find her. She hoped her father wouldn't give the location away. He had shown it to her just yesterday.

Mutter had been tutoring the children about popular games for Americans because they were leaving today for the Port of Hamburg and were then to sail to New York in the United States. It would be a dangerous crossing, but less dangerous than remaining in Berlin with all the restrictions being placed on the Jews. Stories were circulating, horrific stories if they could be believed.

Although Hannah was too old for childish games, she played along for the sake of her brother. *Mutter* had shown her their ultimate destination on a map. She'd never admit it, but hide-and-go-seek was fun. Maybe America wouldn't be so bad after all. Of course, she had protested when she first heard the idea.

"But why do we have to go to America?" Hannah had cried when her mother made the announcement and started the packing process. "I will miss my friends and my home. Why must we leave Germany?" The truth was many of her friends had already left the country.

"Papa says things will just get worse for us in Germany. We will go away until it is safe for us to return."

"You're getting colder," Hannah whispered, as her mother's voice faded. She willed her mother to hear her, but there was no answer.

Hannah startled at the sound of heavy pounding on the door. Her father answered politely in the voice he reserved for company. Formal, insincere. A cool welcome.

"SS Sturmbannführer Hoffman, you're early. We weren't expecting you until tomorrow."

"I'm afraid there's been a change in plans, Herr Hirschfeld. We had to move up the date, and I'm here for the package."

"But, Franz, we had an agreement."

The Sturmbannführer laughed. It was a cruel laugh that resounded in the foyer and carried all the way to Hannah's hiding place.

"I'm here. I kept my part of the bargain. Now I will take delivery of the diamonds."

"But we thought we had until tomorrow to leave."

"I have my orders. I am requisitioning your house, and my men are here to escort your family to the train station."

"And from the station, where?"

"Nothing to be alarmed about. Just to a work camp until we get everything sorted out."

"But my son, he's only a baby, he cannot work. And my wife? And my—"

The Sturmbannführer dismissed him in mid-sentence.

"That, Herr Hirschfeld, is no longer my problem."

"But we shook hands. We had a gentlemen's agreement, did we not?" Herr Hirschfeld said, trying to maintain a calm demeanor. She knew her father was used to conducting business on a handshake. His word was his bond. He had taught her that lesson many times. If a customer wanted a particular piece of jewelry and couldn't pay, they entered into a verbal pact. Herr Hirschfeld would get the money eventually, but the customer could take home the fancy ring for his fiancée or a pearl necklace for his wife or a diamond brooch for his mother.

"I'm afraid I'm not a gentleman," growled the intruder, his voice growing angrier by the minute. "And neither, it seems are you."

The Sturmbannführer looked around. "I see you are all packed up and ready to leave, *a day early*. What would have happened to our agreement if I had arrived on schedule tomorrow? You and your family would be gone, and I would not get my diamonds."

When her father didn't answer, the Sturmbannführer continued. "No matter," he clucked disapprovingly, and Hannah imagined he was reining in his anger with a restrained smile. "Things will work out very nicely after all."

"B-but my family. What will happen to them?" her father stuttered.

Even from her hiding place Hannah could sense her father's nerves by the unnatural pitch of his voice.

"What matter is that to me? Now, where are the diamonds you promised me?"

"I don't have them here," insisted Herr Hirschfeld.

"Of course you do. You've boarded up your shop, and you are about to flee the country with the false papers I provided you and your friends in return for the diamonds. Only you were going to use those papers to escape and take the diamonds with you. Don't try to deny it. I've already picked up other members of your party, and they were eager to talk to save themselves."

The Sturmbannführer directed his men to grab Herr Hirschfeld and his family while he organized the search of the house.

"Julian, what is going on?" Ana cried as she was dragged into the foyer, Aaron sniffling on her hip. "What are these men doing here in our home?"

"I'm afraid your husband has failed to meet his part of the bargain, and now you and your son must pay the consequences."

"Please," begged Herr Hirschfeld. "Take me, but leave my wife and son alone. They did nothing."

"Stop, you're hurting me," Frau Hirschfeld called out, trying to pull away from the man restraining her. Hannah heard a resounding slap and her mother's soft crying. Aaron started wailing and wouldn't be soothed.

"Silence your son, or I'll shoot him," sputtered the Sturmbannführer. "Now search this house, every crevice. Tear it apart if you have to, but find those diamonds."

Hannah shivered. What if they found her? Why didn't Papa give the man the diamonds?

"Take them away. I'll find what I'm looking for in this house. I don't need them. How many hiding places could there be?"

Her father tried to reason with the intruder. "But Herr Sturmbannführer, we can work this out. I will tell you where the diamonds are, and we can forget this unfortunate misunderstanding ever happened."

Hannah hugged her knees and soaked up the sweat from her brow with her shirtsleeves. Surely, the Sturmbannführer could hear her beating heart. It was pounding out of her chest. Something bad was happening. She started to come out of her hiding place to be with her mother. Whatever was going on, she didn't want to face it alone.

She heard her mother's faint voice. "Julian, if we can save one of the children…" There was a pause, and then she heard her mother's voice again, this time rising strongly.

"Don't come out, don't come out, wherever you are," her mother sang in a chirpy falsetto, as if it were part of the song from the game. Hannah couldn't see the scene from her hiding place. She clenched her fists and waited. Did this song hold a message for her?

The Sturmbannführer barked another order. "This woman is insane. Take her away," he said, dismissing her.

"But our luggage," said Herr Hirschfeld.

"You won't need that where you're going." And to his remaining men, the Sturmbannführer ordered,

"Search the house, but don't destroy it. I will be living here from now on."

Two sets of jackboots stomped out of the room and up the stairs, pounding the stairs above Hannah's head. She stayed frozen in place on her mother's orders as her parents and little brother were dragged away. Before she had a chance to tell them she loved them. Not a final hug or a final goodbye. And that was the last time she ever heard her mother's sweet voice or her father's nervous laughter or her brother's booming cry. But she would never forget the strident voice of the man who had taken them.

Chapter Five
Hannah's Story: The Duplicitous Hausfrau

Berlin 1948

It was not difficult to get the Sturmbannführer to notice her. She wasn't practiced at flirting, but she barely had to bat her eyelashes or feign an indecent reveal. He was easy to lead, and once he'd stumbled, it was a short trip to falling in love. He was almost twice her age. And it didn't hurt that she embodied the ideal Aryan woman—blonde, beautiful, and buxom. She was outside his house…formerly *her* house…desperate to get in to see how the place had changed, to see if she could find a trace of her former life or her family.

For a long time, after the war, she had held out hope her parents might still be alive. She posted their names in all the proper places, with every search organization she could find, checked the refugee lists daily, eager to talk to anyone who had been in the camps and ask if they had seen her parents and her little brother. Until one day she saw their names on a list in the archives—the Hirschfeld family—Julian, Ana, and Aaron, all killed the same day, upon their arrival in the Auschwitz extermination center, not long after they had been forcibly taken from their home to the transports. They didn't survive the selection process, but how did they die? Were they lined up and shot? Shot in a crowd trying to get to each other? Hanged? Electrified on the perimeter fence trying to escape? Beaten to death by the SS? Or by the kapos, Jewish prisoners who served as executioners for the Germans, in the killing center? Gassed in the showers and burned in the crematoria? Singled out during one of the frequent random selections?

Many inmates, she knew, fell victim to illness or malnutrition. There was so little food the prisoners literally starved to death. There were many ways to die in the camps. She'd heard every unimaginable story at the displaced persons camp. Her parents' method of death wasn't recorded. She hoped it had been over quickly, that they hadn't suffered too much.

But she didn't really believe the lists until she ran into Madeline Hammerman, her mother's best friend, after the war. Madeline had been to Auschwitz. Her registration number was tattooed on her left forearm. According to the survivors Hannah had spoken to, by the time the last people arrived at the camp, they were no longer identified by name, just their numbers. Madeline had seen Hannah's parents because they'd traveled on the same suffocating railcar to Poland, so she recounted the story. And then Hannah could no longer pretend.

"Your mother was holding your father's hand," Madeline recalled. "Then they were separated. He was sent to the right and she and your baby brother ordered to go to the left, with me. He refused to be parted from her. He tried to reason with the guards, but they couldn't be reasoned with. So he got a bullet in the head for his trouble. Ana lost her will and lost her mind then, and she and Aaron and I were herded into another line with the children, women, and old people. A line where people went and never came back. Your father was the lucky one. It was over for him very quickly."

Madeline's own beloved husband, Abraham, had disappeared into the camp, and she never saw him again. She fancied he had been on a forced labor work detail outside the camp in the coal mines or the rock quarries, on a construction project or at a weapons facility, aiding the German war effort, and had somehow escaped, perhaps joined the resistance. He was a very strong and resourceful man. But she knew that was an unlikely scenario. People didn't escape from Auschwitz.

Madeline was pulled out of the shower line for other things. Unspeakable things. Things she endured for scraps of food and warmth and to stay alive. Things she was so ashamed of doing she felt guilty and unworthy to return to the normal life she knew. "If anybody asks, you never saw me," she said.

The camp had been liberated by Soviet soldiers. The inmates who had stayed behind, mostly the infirm who were at death's door, like Madeline, woke up one day and found the German officers had gone, disappeared. The Russians who liberated the camp said the inmates could stay on or find their way home. Before the camp's liberation, most of the inmates had been forced on a death march, which not many survived.

Madeline was one of the lucky ones. Eventually she made her way back to Berlin, only to find that someone else had taken over the Hammerman house. Since she had no money, no means of support, and no place to go, she ended up at the displaced persons camp. There she met a very kind American soldier—a Jew, in fact. After searching for her husband in vain for months after the war, she had seen his name on a list—not the list of survivors. That's why he hadn't found her. If Abe had been alive, he would have moved heaven and earth to get to her. She was sure of it. She agreed to marry the soldier and move to the United States. That was where Abraham had been planning to take her, so that was where she wanted to go. Before she left, her soldier found Hannah a job as a typist in a small accounting firm. The women had hugged, made the usual promises that they would see each other again. And, indeed, they had kept in touch through the years.

By now, everyone knew the unbelievable truth about what the Germans had done to the Jews. It was no longer just rumor. American soldiers who had freed the skeletal victims had seen the reality with their own eyes. Countless stories appeared in the newspapers. Each survivor had his or her own personal journey, a unique story. Men, women, children. Average Germans gave statements claiming they had no idea what was happening under their own noses, that they were surprised to learn what had happened.

Hannah could blame the SS guards at the camp, the ones who relayed instructions to go left or go right. Or the officers who led the people to the showers like sheep to the slaughter. Or even Hitler himself. Heaven knew there was enough blame to go around. But Hannah held only one person responsible. Sturmbannführer Hoffman. The evil man whose voice was the last she heard before her parents and baby brother disappeared forever. Whose face she imagined in her nightmares. And she was determined to spend the rest of her life making him pay.

Her plan wasn't fully formed. She wasn't entirely sure how she, a mere girl, was going to bring down a monster, a seasoned warrior, but she knew she had to try.

Of course he didn't recognize her. He hadn't seen her at the house that morning. And she had grown since then. But she'd heard his voice. It was unmistakable. She would never forget it. And his name. He hadn't even bothered to change it. He wasn't held accountable in the trials following the war. He was just a minor player, one of many minor players, regular, everyday Germans who had just gone along with what they were calling the Final Solution. He had sent her family and countless others to their deaths, lining his pockets along the way. But he was just following orders—the guilt-assuaging words that were so popular in post-war Germany.

He had requisitioned her home for himself, and he was still living in it. Was there no justice in the world? German officials didn't hold anyone to account. In fact, former Nazis slipped in and out of Germany with impunity. That was the country's dirty little secret. And all the while, government and major corporations, often staffed by former Nazis, looked the other way.

She had been one of the lucky ones, one of the 1,500 Jews who survived the Holocaust hiding in Berlin. She had escaped the roundups. But her life was bleak and meaningless without her family. She should have gone with them that day. She wouldn't have survived, but now, despite being only half alive, really, she was going to take action, to make their lives count for something.

Being a practicing Jew was not a mantle she was ready to reassume. To her neighbors, she was a good Catholic. She continued to go to church with her foster parents. But she was just going through the motions. How could she pray to a God, any God, who would allow the Holocaust to happen?

And then, one day, her opportunity arose when she was standing in front of her old house, peering in the windows.

"See anything interesting in there, Fräulein?"

Hannah froze. His tone was flirtatious, but it was still the voice of her nightmares. And she was caught. She pivoted slowly away from the window.

"I haven't seen you around," he continued. "Let me introduce myself. I am Franz Hoffman. I am the owner of this house."

Hannah cringed. The monster reached for her hand, and when she touched it she feared she might be sick, right there on the pavement. She gulped in a healing breath, which the Sturmbannführer took for shyness and nerves. That seemed to inflame him even more. He had dropped his Sturmbannführer moniker and now he was simply Herr Hoffman, a presentable German businessman with a clean slate, courting a much younger girl.

He looked at her like a hungry leopard about to pounce on his prey. She had been told by many she was beautiful. She had inherited her blonde hair and green eyes from her mother, who had Scandinavian roots. But her mother's Aryan looks hadn't saved her. Hannah had other plans. Hannah had a secret. Her campaign to bring the Sturmbannführer to justice was about to begin.

Herr Hoffman still had hold of her hand. "And you are?"

"Eva," she said, going by the name given her by the family who had hidden and later adopted her.

"A lovely name," he commented. Of course he was thinking of Eva Braun, the mistress, and finally wife, of his hero. "For a lovely girl." And she was barely a girl, just shy of her twentieth birthday, in the bloom of womanhood.

And so began the courtship and the eventual walk down the aisle. Her adoptive parents tried to dissuade her, but she was adamant. This was the man she wanted to marry.

She had been a virgin. There were no prospects for a girl hidden in the attic for years, and when she got out, no Jewish men of appropriate age. Most had been killed during the war. Many German men, too. It was customary to marry an older man. A sign of the times. She had no savings, no means of support other than her work. She hadn't attended school during the war years. Her low-level job in the accounting firm didn't pay much, so she hadn't saved anything.

Of course she had harbored dreams of one day finding true love, of celebrating a wedding night where she and her new husband would enjoy exploring each other's bodies and creating children. She'd had plenty of time to read about love and romance in the dusty attic of her adoptive parents. But postwar Germany was no place for unrealistic dreams.

Once the plan caught hold, she was determined to see it through. And once she was "in the door," his home would be hers once again. But what a personal price to pay for justice.

Herr Hoffman was gallant during the courtship. He took her to fine restaurants, to concerts, on picnics, and to meet his friends and family. He was always on his best behavior. A consummate gentleman, holding the door for her, offering her his jacket on cold nights. There were stolen kisses, yes, but he never made an improper move.

Once they had recited their wedding vows, however, his true nature was revealed. He was not a tender or sensitive lover. He was brutal and cruel, and he left bruises and bites when he used her, wherever he touched her. He was also verbally abusive. But she was back in her home among her parents' things, the beautiful artwork, tapestries, heirloom china and furniture, surrounded once again by the familiar trappings of her family.

Her husband hadn't changed much about the house. She wandered through the ballroom and imagined she heard strains of a waltz at one of her parents' many formal dinner parties. They still dined on her mother's Meissen porcelain, the popular Blue Onion pattern, and the family's fine heirloom linen tablecloths. The first time she wandered into her parents' bedroom, now *her* bedroom, and inspected the drawers, she detected the sweet, powdery vanilla scent of her mother's favorite perfume, Shalimar, and the fragrance of bergamot brought her to tears. How was that possible after five years? She half expected her mother to come down the hall, but, regrettably, she would never see her mother again.

As the months went by, she noticed that the valuable paintings were slowly disappearing from the walls, sold off by her husband. She didn't think it was possible she could hate him more. She didn't think she could tolerate much more of this deception. But her plan was working.

Apparently, despite years of hiding in the dark and deprivation, she was very fertile, because not long after the wedding she showed signs of pregnancy. That was definitely *not* part of the plan. She was bereft. Herr Hoffman was beside himself with joy. To him she was the classic German maiden repopulating the Fatherland. He even mellowed a bit, but became more proprietary and would hardly let her out of his sight. He took every opportunity to pat her stomach, which made her cringe and made him even lustier, as he fondled her swelling breasts at every opportunity and whispered crude innuendos.

One thing was certain. She would not bring a child of her husband's into this world. And she would have to act fast, because this baby was growing by leaps and bounds. Her grief was genuine, but she was conflicted. A monster's spawn was growing inside her, but she wanted so much to have a baby of her own. How could she murder her own child? A child who would carry the essence of her parents. There had been enough killing to last six million lifetimes.

Herr Hoffman demanded sex every night. In fact, he craved it. But when she complained that it wasn't good for the baby, he began to turn to other women. She was grateful for that. She knew he was unfaithful, because when he came home from late night "meetings" his clothes stank of cheap perfume and there was lipstick on the collar of his shirts. Those women were her saviors. They meant she wouldn't have to be pawed and suckled by the depraved man she shared her bed with. And he delighted in telling her of his escapades and what the other women let him do to do them.

Whenever he did force himself upon her, mostly in a drunken stupor, he punished her, perhaps because she was no longer the compliant, sweet-natured, sensual girl he had married. He treated her like one of his whores in the bedroom. On those nights, after those times, she went to the shower and spent hours scrubbing the stink of him off her body.

What would he think if he discovered he had married and was sleeping with a Jewess? Turning the tables on him might make her life almost tolerable.

Each Friday night when he left to meet another woman or to meet his friends, she prepared a Shabbos dinner, with flavorful chicken soup and matzo balls, roast chicken, and a fresh-baked challah to welcome in the Sabbath like her mother taught her. She kept the silver polished until it shone. Right before sundown, she covered her head with a lace cap and lit the candles in her parents' silver candlesticks, which the Sturmbannführer had "acquired" when he appropriated the Hirschfeld home. Then she moved her hands inward in a circular motion three times, covered her eyes, and recited the Sabbath prayer, offering a personal blessing over the souls of her parents and her baby brother.

When she was through eating the meal in silence, she brought the leftover food to a displaced persons camp for refugees and former inmates of Nazi concentration camps. There she ran into Madeline Hammerman, her mother's best friend, who had miraculously survived Auschwitz. And that was how she got by, living for those Friday nights, awash in sweet memories, helping others. The residents of the camps were ghost people, shadows, hovering between life and death, with only hope to keep them tethered to the earth.

Herr Hoffman often spoke of his continuing search for a cache of diamonds. She knew he was talking about her father's diamonds. Apparently they were still hidden somewhere in the house. Hannah had desperately tried but couldn't find them either. Her father had hidden them well, or maybe they really had never been in the house. A lot of good they had done her family or the other families planning to leave the country with them. Her father had betrayed his friends, whose families met the same fate as hers. He wouldn't give up the hiding place of the diamonds, so they had paid with their lives.

But even if she couldn't find the diamonds, she had something better—a hand-copied stack of incriminating documents. Franz was involved in a secret society of ex-SS officers who met on a regular basis at the Hirschfeld house, which was how she thought of it. They called themselves the *Zersetzung Gruppen KG.* Loosely translated, it meant disintegration and dispersal. Dissolution and salvaging of assets and possessions, property, objects of art, bank accounts, gold, silver, and currency. Primarily Jewish assets were being transferred. Not legally transferred, but appropriated through apprehension or seizure, like Herr Hoffman had seized her house and many of the valuable goods inside.

There might once have been hastily drawn contracts, agreed to by desperate people who signed on the dotted line under duress, to gain any amount of money in hopes of escaping their fate. *Zersetzung Gruppen KG* was in the business of appropriations, liquidations, and transfers as if it were a legitimate moving and storage company going about transferring possessions of happy people on the move. And her husband was the ringleader of the group. The head of the snake. The president of the *Gruppen*.

Their intent wasn't to reestablish the Reich or take back Germany. But it was more than just old warriors reminiscing about the good old days. Their motives were more materialistic. Collectively, they had accumulated untold wealth in the form of jewels and money and property and priceless paintings from the families they had terrorized or deported. Few of their victims had survived, so these vultures were in a position to profit from their tragedy. These lesser functionaries of the party had flown below the radar screen of the Allies and escaped the notorious Nuremberg trials. Members of the group infiltrated the government in strategic positions in order to maintain even more control over their ill-gotten gains and enable their comrades to continue to line their pockets with the spoils of war.

They had strategic connections. If a painting of questionable provenance surfaced, the group had an art dealer who was willing to look the other way for a hefty fee. If they came into possession of a fabulous emerald necklace, there was a jeweler on their payroll to facilitate the sale. Specifically, a jeweler who had taken over her father's boarded-up shop and all of the merchandise in it, as easily as her husband had taken possession of her father's house, without benefit of any transaction papers. They controlled banks, corporations, even the secret police. Whether the German government was unaware of their actions or merely complicit, what did it matter? *Zersetzung Gruppen KG* was all-powerful and unstoppable.

Her experience at the accounting firm came in handy. Franz decided to have her sit in on their meetings and take detailed minutes. Over the past weeks and months, she had gathered enough evidence to prosecute this traitorous ring of "pseudo patriots." She took copious notes about where they hid their money, banks they did business with, anything of importance they discussed when they met at her house. She listed every name. Documented every plan. Copied every account number. Recorded the sale of every stolen painting. Some of which she recognized from the homes of her parents' friends. One in particular was a Degas painting of ballet dancers. Madeline Hammerman was a French ballet dancer, and the Hammermans had prized that painting.

All the while she served as the group's secretary, she was also cooking their meals and tolerating their foul-smelling pipe smoke and their bawdy jokes. Her husband allowed his friends to paw her at will. The beasts grew lustier with every stein of beer they consumed. They had little respect for a pregnant woman—or any woman, for that matter.

But what she had discovered would be worth the cost. In the end, though, who could she report her findings to? Who could she trust? Certainly not the German government, which had abdicated its responsibility and plunged her country into a devastating economic death spiral and now seemed to be protecting the very people who were responsible for the reign of terror against its citizens. She couldn't approach a newspaper. Who knew its real sentiments? Behind every benign German mask, every façade, she saw the face of evil. To the outside world, the members of the *Gruppen* appeared contrite, but alone, in their conclave, she detected no evidence of regret. Deep down, these men hadn't changed at all.

Maybe she could take the damaging documents to the Israelis? She didn't know any of those. Israel was a fledgling faraway land she could never hope to get to. Groups of Jews were reportedly being smuggled into Palestine, but she had no money of her own to make the journey. Herr Hoffman kept a close watch on her and permitted her only enough money to maintain the household. She was, after all, his property. He wouldn't let her out of the house to work. He had forced her to quit her job because she might come into contact with people who would fill her head with ideas. So, in a way, she was trapped, in hiding again, just like she had been during the miserable, dark war years, a virtual prisoner in her own home.

When she had accumulated enough evidence against her husband and his friends, she contemplated her exit plan. She dreamed of escaping. But how? She could kill Herr Hoffman in his sleep, or poison his food. As his widow, she might inherit his house, her family's house. But was she capable of murder? She doubted it, although she had imagined it dozens of times in her head. She had visions of poisoning the traitorous lot of them, perhaps in the food or the wine she served them. She would be generous with the tainted portions. Meanwhile her belly was growing larger as her options grew smaller.

Could she wait for her husband to grow old and die? She didn't want to spend one more minute, much less one more night, with this disgusting man she had married. Perhaps she could arrange for him to suffer a serious, unexpected accident.

In the end, she couldn't stand to be in his presence a moment longer. And she wanted to get rid of his child, but abortions were illegal throughout Germany. She could have gone to the Netherlands, but she decided to go to Switzerland. Much as she hated her husband, she had come to the conclusion she couldn't end the life she was carrying.

She took a stack of money from one of her husband's hiding places, packed an overnight bag with the documents she had collected and her mother's silver candlesticks, and boarded the train to Switzerland, where the story of her life began. Exhausted, she went to a hotel near the train station, but there were no vacancies. Too tired to go on, she rested on a bench in a park by the lake and fell asleep. She awoke in the morning, cold, her face tear-stained, wondering what to do next.

A man walking his dog came by and asked what was wrong. She had nowhere else to turn. She was a virtual stranger in this country. He was well dressed, sympathetic, and had understanding eyes. So he sat down on the bench beside her, and she told him everything about her predicament. It turned out this man was a prosperous Swiss banker. He dried her eyes with his handkerchief and told her that every life was precious in God's eyes and agreed she should keep the child.

'"And how will I raise him or her?"

"We will find a way." Right then and there, she fell in love with Hans-Peter Grandcoeur. He was a good provider and a tender lover and partner. She moved in with him, told him she couldn't marry him because legally she was still married. They were blessed with four children of their own in addition to the Sturmbannführer's son, and they had a very happy life up until the day her beloved "husband" died. She didn't regret a moment of her life with him.

PART THREE

*THE ADVENTURES OF
PARKER, POLLY,
ALEXANDER AND HALLELUJAH*

Marilyn Baron

Chapter Six
Sailing Toward the Baltic Sea
Hallelujah and Alexander

Present Day

AS THE PLANET SPINS SCRIPT EXTRACT
BY HALLELUJAH WEISS
SCENE 3. ABOARD A LUXURY YACHT CHARTER IN THE MEDITERRANEAN SEA.
PARKER: It's all arranged, then.
POLLY: What's arranged?
PARKER: I've spoken to the captain. We're to be married aboard ship. It will be our most incredible wedding yet. We'll be stopping at the most exotic ports—the French Riviera, the Italian Coast, and Greece.
POLLY: [SIGHING] Those places sound lovely, but as usual, you're getting ahead of yourself. I haven't accepted your proposal.
PARKER: But you're wearing my ring.
POLLY: [ADMIRES THE FLASH OF THE EMERALD-CUT DIAMOND IN AN ANTIQUE PLATINUM SETTING ON HER FINGER] I do love the ring, Parker, but I haven't decided to take you back.
PARKER: Polly, what can I do to convince you? How can I make it up to you? I've already told you I was sorry I slipped.

POLLY: Slipped? You make it sound like you accidentally stumbled over a piece of furniture instead of breaking my heart. You cheated on me, Parker, again. I don't know how much more of it I can take.
PARKER: And yet you still love me, because you know we were meant to be together.
POLLY: You don't make it easy to love you, Parker. When I think of all those other women. I used to believe in destiny, but not anymore.
PARKER: You're the only woman for me, Pollyanna.

****

Hallelujah put the finishing touches on her latest script and catapulted it into cyberspace. Officially, she was still on vacation, but this creative burst of energy could not be denied. The new pages represented some of her best work yet, and she could hardly wait to share it with her boss. The cruise would provide plenty of fodder for future episodes.

The response from California was swift. The executive producer, the head writer, and the show's creator loved the idea of Parker and Polly patching things up on a romantic ocean cruise and a wedding on the high seas. The timing was perfect for the February Sweeps. They would take *As the Planet Spins* on the road. The whole cast would be written into the plot, from the cream of Milano society to the chief of police. But Hallelujah wasn't sure Polly was ready to take her errant husband back. She wanted to make him pay. There would be no smooth sailing for Parker. Secrets from Parker's past would be revealed. That would keep the viewers on the hook.

"The ship will be rolling slightly in the sea. Enjoy the departure from wonderful Copenhagen." The captain's voice crackled through the in-room channel broadcasting into their suite. He followed this public announcement with a navigation and weather update interspersed with points of interest about their next port of call.

Hallelujah, hardly winded after the Panoramic Copenhagen with Less Walking tour (she and Polly preferred to ride the tour bus), looked at the leftover foreign currency on the bedspread. "How many Danish *Krone* to the dollar again?"

Alexander stepped into the suite from the balcony and flashed a wide grin. He was good with numbers. Ask him any question about a currency or an economic principle, and he was your man. When it came to demystifying the wonder of women, in particular the wonder that was Hallelujah, not so much.

"Now, there's where I shine. If the rate is 50 *DKK*, that's about seven dollars."

"I hate math."

"You can't hate math. Math makes sense. It is supremely logical. You probably just don't understand it."

"Exactly. That's why I hate it. And I don't want to understand it. I got a D in geometry in the fifth grade. I don't need math to do what I do."

"Math is fascinating."

"If you say so. How many more miles until we get to Visby?"

"Two hundred and eighty nautical miles. To convert to statute miles, multiply nautical miles by 1.15."

Knowing that fact seemed to make Alexander ecstatic. TMI. But whatever floats your boat, or rather, ship. She picked up the ship's daily newsletter and read about the city that was called "Gotland's jewel in the crown" and "the city of ruins and roses." She liked roses, but ruins not so much.

Funny, she'd never even heard of Visby. It was apparently somewhere in Sweden. She read the description: "The island of Gotland is considered by many to be one of Northern Europe's most lovely. A mere fifty-five miles from the Swedish mainland, Gotland is richly forested, dotted with medieval towers, and blessed with a climate that is the envy of its neighbors." *Not exactly a tourist haven. More like a home for Viking detritus.* And she was sure there would be saunas. Just what she needed to see, another sauna. The Scandinavians were crazy about them. It seemed that every home had one. Roasting in saunas was apparently a family sport.

"What kind of money do we need in Sweden?"

"The Swedish *Krona (SEK),*" said Alexander. "And remember, we're sailing into a new time zone tonight, so we need to set our clocks and watches an hour forward."

"Is there anything you don't know?"

"I know everything we need to know," answered Alexander, placing a firm grip on Hallelujah's hand. "Now let's explore the ship."

"Aren't you afraid someone will see us?"

"That's the beauty of my plan. No one knows we're here."

"You said you were being followed. Could you be mistaken?"

"No. I'm not imagining it. I don't have much of an imagination. The hedge fund business is pretty cut-and-dried. 'What's up?' "

"What do you mean, 'What's up?' "

"It's a joke. Come on. 'What's up?' "

"Okay, 'What's up?' "

"The stock market."

Hallelujah stared blankly at Alexander.

"Just a bit of hedge fund humor."

Hallelujah didn't find the joke the least bit funny. Apparently it appealed to his German sense of humor.

A stampede rushed past the corridor and stomped onto the stairs outside their cabin.

Alexander turned toward the door. "What was that? It sounded like a bunch of banshees."

"It's Ivan the Terrible, his brother Vlad the Impaler, and his other brother Vlad," Hallelujah announced. She'd already given names to the horde of unruly children.

"Does the whole family live in the next cabin?"

"I think it's two families, cousins and aunts and uncles, and they're taking up the two rooms on either side of us. But the parents are nowhere to be seen. They're letting their kids run wild."

"Do you think they're the ones who rang our bell in the middle of the night?"

"My guess is yes." Hallelujah squeezed his hand. "Let's go up to Palm Cove and have afternoon tea."

Hallelujah and Alex took the elevator to the top deck, where a jazz band was playing. The server hovered nearby, waiting to take their order as the ship slowly pulled out of the harbor of Denmark's capital, largest city, and largest port. The union mark, the Danish royal coat of arms, was flying, its blue background with three gold crowns clear against a burnished sky. It was a beautiful evening.

A sultry singer in a silky chartreuse knee-length dress and black heels sang and swayed as the jazz band played "I've Got Rhythm," "True Love," and "Witchcraft," followed by "I Love Her." This was the kind of music Hallelujah enjoyed and that her father had taught her to dance to.

She studied the menu and gave her order to the server. "I'll have the verbena mint organic tea."

Alexander ordered a light beer.

Birds glided across the sun-kissed sea, which sparkled like diamonds. Like the diamonds Alexander was storing in their stateroom.

"Do you want to dance?" Alexander asked.

Hallelujah nodded, and they took to the floor.

They were playing "Till," one of her favorite songs by The Vogues. "You are my reason to live…" she sang to herself, and hugged Alexander tighter. There was something about that song. It was over-the-top romantic. And the boy had moves. He was smooth, like Parker. When the song was almost over, she whispered against his cheek, "You're a good partner."

Alexander flushed. Most girls considered him dull as dirt, a less than exciting companion, not worth a second look.

"You'll have to thank my mother for that. Mom taught me to dance before I came over here, in case I got an opportunity to dance with a beautiful woman in Berlin."

Hallelujah's face colored at the compliment. He thought she was beautiful. She hadn't heard that for a long time. The more discouraged she was about her own life, the more emotion she poured into her scripts, which was why Parker and Polly sizzled on the small screen. She was beginning to feel something for Alexander, but she didn't quite trust it. It was too soon after her own debacle of a marriage. Maybe she was jumping back into the frying pan prematurely. A good way to get burned, again. Every time she thought about Lloyd and his betrayal, she seethed. Why hadn't she seen it coming? Was she so involved with Parker and Polly that she couldn't see the forest for the trees? Had she let Lloyd get away? Was she somehow responsible for their breakup? Maybe she wasn't enough to satisfy her own husband. Or was Lloyd just a shallow horndog?

Alexander whirled her around the dance floor. "Why did your parents name you Hallelujah?"

Still moving in his arms, she answered, "Aside from the obvious fact that my father is a rabbi, he told me once that every life in the Holocaust comes back in the spirit of another human being. There was a picture of a little girl in a Holocaust Museum he had visited in Europe that haunted him long after he'd left the continent. Her name was Hallelujah. He named me for her. Perhaps I'm her sister spirit, the sister of her soul."

"That's a lovely thought."

"Also, my parents didn't think they could have children, so when I finally came along, I was their miracle. The name just seemed to fit."

Alexander danced them back to their seats by the picture window, where a plate of scones, both plain and raisin, was waiting, along with clotted cream and a mixture of fruit. Hallelujah steeped her teabag and stirred in two packages of brown sugar crystals.

"I don't know how we'll ever figure out who we

should return those diamonds to," Alexander said before he bit into his scone.

Hallelujah had been mulling over the matter ever since Alexander had told her about finding the cache of gems in his house during the remodeling project.

"Mr. Hedge Fund Manager, did you ever think to track down the person who paid for the stumble stones in honor of the Hirschfeld family? Follow the money trail?"

Alexander placed his scone on the dessert plate in front of him. "That's a great idea. Why didn't I think of that? We'll do that as soon as we get back to the room, if the Internet connection is working."

Hallelujah's eyes followed the dips and swells of the waves, whitecap spray under a darkening sky. Totally relaxed in her wing chair, she swayed to the tug and pull of the ship as it sliced across the sea. From her seat in the lounge, she observed the sea traffic and the glitter of lights from other ships. The scene had a magical, romantic quality. Alexander had a speck of clotted cream on his upper lip that she wanted to lick off or wipe away, but it seemed too forward.

She knew next to nothing about the man, except that he was devilishly handsome, if not a tad bit proper and still hurting from Sigrid's betrayal. He was nothing like Lloyd. But she wanted to know more. Something about him spoke to her. Something magnetic. She was falling for a man she hardly knew.

"Tell me something about yourself that most people don't know," Hallelujah posed.

"Let me see," began Alexander. "When I was growing up, I wanted to be in a band."

"Did you have a particular musical talent?"

"No, but I remembered that story about the orchestra that played on the deck of the *Titanic* as it went down."

Hallelujah laughed. "You have a strange sense of humor bringing that up while we're in the middle of the Baltic." But she secretly considered him brave to want to distract the passengers on the doomed ship.

Alexander reached for Hallelujah's hand to help her out of her chair. The spark sizzled like an electric connection.

"Let's go back to the room and get ready for dinner. I know how much you like Italian food. I can't take you to Italy, but we're going to eat in the Italian specialty restaurant."

Hallelujah was up for that. Her love affair with pasta had begun when she studied abroad in Florence, Italy, during her senior year in college. Since then, she'd been in search of the perfect dish of pasta. An eternal optimist, she hoped she would find it tonight. Most restaurants were extreme disappointments. Cooks in the U.S. weren't great at *al dente* and were heavy handed with the cream sauce. She and Polly preferred linguine and white clam sauce or spaghetti *aglio e olio*. Polly was *molta cosmopolitana.*

Was she also looking for the perfect man? She'd been disappointed before. Could this be the start of a love affair?

Alexander continued to hold her hand as they waited for the elevator that would take them to their suite. He'd insisted on holding hands and stealing kisses when they were in public to give credence to the idea that they were a real couple. And even though she was playing a role, she melted at his drugging kisses and wanted more.

The "hordes" rushed by them down the staircase, making a ruckus as they went and breaking into her reverie.

"I hope they wear themselves out so they don't disturb us tonight," Alexander commented as he opened the door to their suite.

"What's tonight?" Hallelujah asked.

"You'll see," he said, smiling broadly.

With Alexander you always knew where you stood. He was an open book, not good at hiding his emotions.

It was hard to maneuver in their ridiculously ship-sized bathroom, which she knew was larger than most, since it was reserved for honeymooners. At least there were two sinks. After her failed marriage, Hallelujah had discovered she liked having her own space.

She couldn't remember the last time she had applied makeup or undressed in front of someone who wasn't Lloyd. Now, alone in the room with Alexander, she was self-conscious.

When she'd first entered the suite, the first thing she noticed was the bed, which played a starring role in the room. Luckily, it was huge, but it was also round, and there was a mirror above it. Where did Alexander think he was going to bunk? What did he have in mind? It turned out he was going to bunk with her, but he kept pretty much to his side of the circular bed. Lloyd, like Parker, was a bed hog.

She should have seen the train wreck that was Lloyd coming. But she'd had faith in Lloyd's fidelity—or maybe she didn't care enough after she found out. Someone had to be blamed for the breakup, and she preferred to blame Lloyd, although that hussy Liv could have instigated it. Even their names sounded right together. Liv and Lloyd. Liv's foot was the perfect fit to Prince Lloyd's glass slipper. Did he call her by a pet name—Livvie or Livia—or better yet, her whole name, Olivia? No, that took too much time, and Lloyd was always in a hurry.

Alexander looked over at Hallelujah while he shaved. "I never asked what you do for a living."

"I write for a soap opera."

"As the Wind Blows?"

"Ha. Ha. It's actually *As the Planet Spins*."

"No, seriously, I like soap operas. My grandmother used to watch a show, and she got me hooked. I think it was called *The Old and the Infirm*."

"Laugh all you want. Our show has some of the highest ratings in Berlin. I'm surprised you never heard of it."

"No, really, I didn't mean to make light of it. It sounds like interesting work. But I don't have time to watch soap operas."

Hallelujah nodded her agreement as she finished applying her makeup.

"It must be confusing to write for all those characters—keeping them all straight."

"No, actually I only write dialogue for the two central characters, Parker and Polly Winthrop. I know them intimately. I know what they're thinking before they do. As a matter of fact, whenever I'm in an awkward social situation and at a loss for words, I crawl inside my characters' heads and imagine what Polly would say."

Hallelujah could write Parker and Polly out of any

situation, but somehow she hadn't been able to write a happy ending to her own disastrous marriage. Parker and Polly had been through a lot—marriages, remarriages to themselves and others, affairs, pregnancies, comas, and kidnappings, and they always ended up back together. When push came to shove, after the failure of her own marriage, Hallelujah did the most unimaginative thing she could. She bolted. And now she was running for her life.

What if Parker and Polly were being chased by unknown killers? How would they handle it?

Hallelujah tapped her chin and studied her reflection in the mirror. They'd probably do what Alexander had done. Hop aboard a luxury cruise ship and sail away. It was epic Parker and Polly.

Alexander interrupted her reverie. "And after dinner, we're going to be married in the ship's chapel."

Hallelujah spun around, nearly knocking Alexander into the shower stall. He grabbed hold of the white curtains and the towel bar and caught himself in time.

"What did you say?"

"Weren't you listening? I said we're going to get married."

"Married?" she sputtered.

"I told you that was the plan," Alexander said. "The ship is registered in Moldavia. Therefore, the captain can marry us without a license in international waters."

"Is that legal?"

"It is."

Hallelujah placed her hand on Alexander's arm and breathed in his scent. "You know this isn't for real, don't you?"

He shrugged. "It's going to happen, unless the ship gets boarded by pirates."

Hallelujah expelled a breath. Alexander was very sure of himself. "Polly got kidnapped by pirates once. Then the twin sister no one knew she had took her place, and it took Parker quite a number of episodes to discover he was sleeping with the wrong sister. Not so uncommon in the soaps."

Alexander smiled.

"Are you making fun of me again?"

"No, actually, I'm intrigued and turned on. My life is pretty boring. Money, stocks, bonds, ups, downs. This is the most fun I've had in ages."

"Since Sigrid, you mean?"

"I don't want to talk about her."

"Speaking of aging, I remember when Polly's daughter, Vanessa, was six years old. She went away to boarding school in Switzerland and when she came back to her hometown of Milano, she was a hormonal teenager. It's what we call Rapid Aging Syndrome in the business."

"Have Parker and Polly ever gotten married aboard a ship?"

"Not since I've been writing them, but I'm going to incorporate that story line into the script. Art imitates life."

"Well, I've arranged our wedding with the Master Captain and the ship's event coordinator. We're even going to have live ceremony music and decorations, including a monogrammed aisle runner and a bridal bouquet. And a cake. Oh, and they're going to decorate our cabin. And we get a bottle of champagne and two keepsake flutes."

"Nice," murmured Hallelujah as she hurried out of the bathroom. Was this really happening?

"They threw in a photographer."

Hallelujah turned around slowly and nodded. "Mmm."

"There was a sleek modern black-and-white option, a tea party-inspired option, a beachy option, and a traditional white wedding option," Alexander rambled. "I chose the traditional because I thought you were a traditional kind of girl."

"I like traditional."

"And sure, I know it's not for real," Alexander conceded. "So, no commitment. That's the catch. Any marriages performed by the captain are valid for the duration of the voyage only."

"That's good, since we hardly know each other."

"Of course, we could follow up and have a legal ceremony when we get home." Alexander hesitated, adding, "If we want to."

Hallelujah's raised an eyebrow, signaling that he was pushing it. She took a deep breath and filled herself with air…and hope.

Was Alexander potential husband material? Could he squash bugs and scoop hair out of the drain? Could he fix a leaky faucet? Was he callous or cuddly? Could he be counted on? It might be interesting to find out. Parker was the type of man to sweep a woman off her feet, not the type to sweep up in the kitchen. Alexander seemed to be taking a page from Parker's book. And she was taking a page from Polly's book.

If she had time to think, it would be interesting to analyze why she was so eager to fall back into her familiar pattern before the ink was even dry on her divorce papers. She and Polly would have to be on their guard.

Chapter Seven
Alexander

He was rushing her, and he knew it. But the idea of marriage was very appealing. Maybe if they tied the knot aboard ship, and spent the next week living together in such close quarters, she would get used to the idea. Although he'd kissed her plenty, always when other people were around, to keep up the pretense, he was not acting a part. He had developed real feelings for Hallelujah.

He didn't delude himself that they would be lovers just because they had a wedding certificate, although he wouldn't have objected to that turn of events.

Hallelujah was sophisticated. She wrote dialogue for glamorous soap opera characters. Why would she be interested in hooking up with a boring hedge fund manager? Obviously Sigrid hadn't been. Did Sigrid ever have feelings for him, or had he been just a placeholder until she could get back together with her ex-husband?

And Hallelujah's ex-husband sounded like a jerk. He wouldn't blame her for not wanting to get involved with anyone ever again. But it had been wonderful sharing a meal with her at *Focaccia's* last night. Looking across the table, seeing her laugh and gush over her linguine with white clam sauce, cooked *al dente*, just the way she liked it, he finally belonged to someone, and specifically to her.

She seemed to have a lot in common with the Polly character she wrote for. She claimed to follow Polly's lead, but from where he sat, Hallelujah was the director, the master of her own destiny. She fed Polly her lines, for heaven's sake. Polly was nothing without Hallelujah. But that's not the way she saw it. With Hallelujah, it was Polly this and Polly that. It was obvious she idolized Polly. But Polly's character fueled Hallelujah's insecurities. Why couldn't she see she had so much more to offer?

Since he'd first laid eyes on her, Hallalujah was all he could see. She was the woman for him. He had no doubts about it.

Why had he chosen her, of all the passengers aboard the Alitalia flight? What was it about her? For one, she looked as if she could be trusted. Two, she was approachable. Three, she was drop-dead gorgeous. All that smooth sable brown hair flowing around her shoulders and those stunning blue eyes. He could hardly look away. She was one of those girls who didn't realize how beautiful she was. Four, she was three sheets to the wind. That's what he needed. Someone who wasn't thinking straight. Otherwise, why would she have gone off on a motorcycle with him, a virtual stranger? Or a cruise, for that matter. Lucky for him she had succumbed. He had to give Polly and her adventurous spirit some of the credit. Certainly.

He didn't think his good fortune was just luck. It was more like fate. He'd walked up and down the aisle of the plane in coach, checking out faces. Nothing. Then he'd sneaked through the curtain to Business Class, and suddenly, there she was. He knew as soon as he laid eyes on her that she was the one. And tomorrow they would walk down the aisle. Maybe then their story would begin.

He didn't kid himself that it was forever. Just until they got out of international waters. But now that he had gotten to know her, he wanted forever. He just had to convince her. He had acted like he was in control, whisking her off on his motorcycle and onto a cruise ship, but the more time she spent with him the sooner she'd learn how rudderless and dull he really was. Hardly a word came out of his mouth that wasn't investment speak. Sometimes, he even bored himself. Compared to the debonair Parker, he was a loser.

Plus, he was playing a dangerous game, and now he'd involved her. He shouldn't have done that. But he wouldn't change a thing. He was just going to have to keep her safe, whatever it took.

Chapter Eight
Alexander and Hallelujah

Alexander and Hallelujah sat shoulder to shoulder at the desk in their honeymoon suite. Although why anyone would need a desk on their honeymoon was confounding. But since their honeymoon was essentially a sham, a desk was rather convenient. Alexander had already checked the stateroom safe, again, to confirm that the diamonds were in there.

Hallelujah was still wearing the white suit he had purchased for her at the onboard boutique. She looked amazing. He couldn't help stealing frequent glances at her as his fingers slid feverishly across the keyboard. She was still wearing one of the flowers from her bridal bouquet in her hair. He resisted the urge to tuck a recalcitrant curl behind her ear, just for the feel of it. She was also wearing the platinum wedding band he'd picked out in the jewelry boutique onboard, another authentic touch. She had to be the most beautiful bride on the planet. And she was *his* bride, at least for the remainder of the cruise.

The ship's technology concierge had configured his wireless-capable laptop with software and full-time connectivity to the Internet so he and Hallelujah could access the ship's network services from the privacy of their stateroom. In his business, he had to be connected to the world at all times, but he'd requested an exclusive ship e-mail address so he could communicate undetected. He was convinced that someone was monitoring his work and personal e-mails. Hallelujah was busy hammering out another script for Parker and Polly.

A bottle of 2005 Louis Roederer Cristal Rosé champagne was chilling in a silver bucket at the far end of the table. They'd already had several glasses of champagne at a celebratory dinner at the ship's specialty steak restaurant. He planned to toast his bride later, and, if he got lucky, steal a kiss or two or more. He wasn't drunk enough to think she would agree to consummate their marriage, but a guy could always hope. She was already a little bit tipsy. And he was head over heels in love with her. Maybe it was the champagne loosening his inhibitions, but he didn't think so. He'd never felt this way about a woman in his life. Not even Sigrid. In fact, Sigrid was slowly slipping from his consciousness. Whenever he closed his eyes and tried to imagine her, the only face he could conjure up was Hallelujah's.

He *had* kissed her after the captain pronounced them man and wife, and his reaction was off the charts. He hoped she'd felt something similar. It was their first post-nuptial kiss, and he didn't want it to end, but she had pulled away just when he was warming up. Was it reluctance he'd read on her face, disappointment, or surprise? He wasn't going to ask her in front of the captain and the witness, who he thanked before they walked out of the chapel on a white runner strewn with red rose petals.

"Your idea about tracking down the person who paid for the stumble stones was a great one. I'm accessing the database now."

Hallelujah pressed her hands together. She would like to spend some time perusing the S*tolpersteine* database, learning the stories of the victims of the Holocaust—her people. She intended to do the research for her novel. Ever since Alexander had shared the story of the stumble stones outside his house, she had been intrigued and decided that the stumble stones would be the theme for the book. But she needed a story, a personal story, to put a face to the tragedy. Right now, Alex was only interested in one family—the Hirschfelds.

"I found them," Alexander said after a fifteen-minute search, reading the screen silently. Hallelujah moved closer, nudging his shoulder. "Apparently, Julian Hirschfeld was a well-known, highly regarded jeweler in Berlin. He ran a business that had been in his family for generations. He was the jeweler to various wealthy, noble, and royal families throughout Europe. It says here the Queen of England had been a regular client. He had a very lucrative business. Married Ana Brinker from Stockholm. He and Ana had two children, Hannah and Aaron. The family was deported to Auschwitz and died there soon after they arrived, in 1943. A woman named Eva Grandcoeur paid for the memorial stones. I wonder who she was? A relative, maybe?"

"Does it give an address for her?"

"Yes, it's in Baden, Switzerland, which is a big wellness destination, known for its hot springs. She lives in some kind of inpatient clinic with thermal springs on *Bäderstrasse*, sort of an oasis with sauna, steam bath, cool room, and thermal bath, and a wide selection of massages." The idea of getting Hallelujah naked and alone in a thermal bath heated his blood. Maybe she'd go for a couples massage. He envisioned them soaping each other down in the bathtub. They were married, after all.

He cleared his throat. "We'll, uh, make a stop in Switzerland as soon as we debark from the ship. We can fly from Stockholm to Zurich and then take the train to Baden. Although you can't always count on the schedule."

"Don't the trains always run on time in Germany?"

"That's a common misconception. And besides, we're talking about Switzerland. Eva Grandcoeur must have some connection with the Hirschfelds. She may know if they have any surviving relatives. I feel that we're getting closer to solving this mystery."

"Are the diamonds still in the room safe?"

Alexander's eyes glanced at the set of drawers where the personal safe was located. He'd had an option of leaving them in a complimentary safe deposit box at the reception desk, but although his package was of special value, he felt better about keeping it stored in the safe in their suite, which he checked obsessively.

"Last time I checked."

Hallelujah laughed and checked the time on her cell phone. "Which was what, ten minutes ago? You're definitely paranoid, Alexander. No one on this ship even knows you have them."

"Well, someone knows. The night I brought the diamonds home from the jeweler's, my house was robbed. That wasn't a coincidence. Luckily, I had dropped them off in my safe deposit box at the bank, or they'd be gone. And ever since then someone has been following me. Like I told you at Fiumicino, someone took a shot at me before I left for the Berlin-Tegel airport. I think I have reason to be paranoid. Do you know how much those rocks are worth?"

"I know you know *exactly* how much they're worth, since you had them appraised. Probably a small fortune. But they're consuming your life."

"The diamonds were found in my house, and they belonged to living, breathing people. A family whose lives were viciously snuffed out. I'm sure it had something to do with why those diamonds were hidden. That family deserves justice, and I'm going to get it for them. I feel obligated."

"You don't have to tell me about obligation," Hallelujah agreed. "I'm a rabbi's daughter. I was raised on a steady diet of the Holocaust. That's why I'd never step foot in Berlin. I don't know how you can live there."

"Hallelujah, I'm German."

"I thought you were American."

"I was born in America. My mother and father were German. Berlin is a wonderful place. I'd love to show you my house after we get this all sorted out."

"There's no way I'm ever going to Berlin."

Alexander frowned. "Berlin has an unfortunate reputation, with the Nazis, and the Cold War, the Wall, and everything."

"You'd better not tell your parents you married a Jewish girl," she challenged.

"Now you're being ridiculous. That wouldn't make a bit of difference to them."

"Well, it would to my parents. It's a good thing this marriage is a sham."

Alexander blew out a breath. "You're not even giving it a chance. We haven't even—"

"Haven't even what—slept together?" Hallelujah stood up abruptly and moved as far away from Alexander as she could get within the confines of the suite. "You're starting to believe this fantasy. You think we're really married, don't you?"

"I have the proof right in the pocket of my jacket," he said, fingering the marriage certificate the captain had provided.

"You're delusional if you think I'm going to sleep with you. You're just a stranger I met on an airplane. I'm going to get off at the next port and fly back to Italy to start my new life."

Alexander got up from the office chair and came around to the back of Hallelujah's seat.

"Hallelujah," he said softly, rubbing her arm. "There was a reason I chose you on that airplane. It was meant to be."

Hallelujah shook her head. "I used to believe in fate. I don't anymore—and don't come any closer." She rose from the chair, walked away from him, and sat on the bed. He followed and sat down beside her.

"Don't you feel anything when I kiss you?"

Hallelujah didn't answer. If she had answered, she might have said, "I feel an explosion and I see stars."

"I know you did, and I'm going to kiss you again," he announced as he put his arms around her.

"Don't," she warned, without much conviction, leaning into him.

He took that as a positive signal. "Hallelujah, I'm not Lloyd, and I'm not Parker. I would never hurt you or break your heart."

Hallelujah frowned. Alexander brought his lips up to hers and coaxed her mouth open. "Kiss me. Kiss me like you mean it." He teased her tongue and kissed her harder. Her arms went around him, and she returned his kiss with a passion that surprised them both.

"I'm not the type of girl who…"

"You're the best type of girl," Alexander whispered. "You're my girl." He placed the palm of his hand on her cheek and rubbed her back in a steady rhythm.

She melted against him. He removed her white jacket and started to unbutton her blouse. Her nipples hardened. He reached under her blouse and massaged her breasts. Hallelujah sighed. She was sinking deeper into the fantasy, buying into the fairy tale of *It Could Happen.*

"I think I've had too much to drink." *Always a good fallback line.*

"I don't think you've had nearly enough." He cupped one breast and deepened the kiss.

Should I stop him? Do I even want to? Polly, what are we getting ourselves into?

Chapter Nine
Julian Grandcoeur

He was named for his grandfather, Julian, although the way his mother talked about her father, she didn't seem to think much of the man. Then again, she didn't seem to think much of her own son. The way she looked at him, as if she were expecting a monster to spring from his body at any moment. Always judging him. Always looking for a flaw. Always disappointed in something he did or said. Her indifference was not overt. But a child could tell whether he was truly loved.

On the other hand, she doted on his half-brother and sisters. She adored them, with their straight blonde hair and blue eyes like their Scandinavian grandmother, Ana Brinker Hirschfeld. When he wanted to know more about her side of the family, she became secretive. But she had named his younger brother after her brother Aaron, and one of his sisters after her beloved mother, Ana. That was all he needed to know.

Sometimes he felt like an odd duck to his siblings' swans, like he didn't belong in the family. He was short, dark, squat, and moody, what his teachers called "rough around the edges." Eva's other children were tall, lithe, and graceful. He was sure he must have been adopted. In fact, it was something of a family joke. And then, when he was forty, she finally admitted the truth. He was fathered by another man, not Hans-Peter

Grandcouer. She hadn't wanted to tell him, but he had been in a skiing accident and his father, his *stepfather*, was eager to donate blood, but his blood wasn't a match.

From the moment he'd learned of his true identity, he'd had the urge to meet his real father. His mother said she hadn't heard from him since the war. She didn't know if he lived in East Berlin or West Berlin, or if he was even living at all, for that matter. She didn't sound as if she cared. They'd had quite a row about it.

"You just left him, pregnant with his child, and ran off without a word?"

His mother didn't seem repentant.

"I did what I had to do."

"Did you ever love him?"

"I'm sorry to say I despised him for every moment of our marriage."

"And did you despise me too?"

Eva inhaled a breath and cast her eyes down. "You are my child. Of course not." But they both knew she was lying.

"Tell me about him. Tell me about my real father, the man you stole from me, the life you stole from me."

"You look just like him." She had pursed her lips, in distaste, as if deciding how much more she wanted to reveal. But he had insisted.

According to his mother, his father had been an evil man, a Nazi SS officer, who had sent her family to the death chamber. The truth hit him like a missile launcher. Not so much that his father was a Nazi but that he had Jewish blood running through his veins.

"I'm sure my father was just following orders like all the rest of the German people during the war."

His mother reared up and slapped him, the first time she'd ever raised her hand to him.

"Following orders? You don't really believe that, do you? You are just like him."

Julian rubbed his cheek where she'd struck him. "I don't know what to believe. You've been lying to me my whole life."

From then on he refused to speak to his mother until she revealed the entire truth, the name of his real father, and where they'd last lived. After he recovered from his skiing accident, he stole money from her purse and from her hiding place in the kitchen, cashed in all of his savings, and took the train to Berlin. After all, she owed it to him. And he was on a mission.

From there, it wasn't difficult to track down Herr Hoffman. His father was overjoyed to see him, stunned to learn that he had been married to a Jewess, was actually still married to her, furious to find out exactly who she was and that his wife was living with another man and had another family in Switzerland. He was convinced she had stolen the diamonds from the house when she left.

It was a tearful reunion. His mother had been right. He was the image of his father and, for the first time in his life, he began to feel comfortable in his own skin. Strong and invincible. Fierce and unapologetic.

His father was no longer living in the house in Dahlem. He'd sold that property and moved on to a more impressive mansion. But he never stopped talking about the lost fortune in diamonds that he believed was or had been in the house. After many years, he had given up on that dream, realizing Julian Hirschfeld must have been telling the truth, that he didn't have the diamonds in his home that morning he came for the family or that Eva, the woman he thought had been his wife, had most likely stolen them when she left him.

But Julian's mother hadn't mentioned anything about diamonds, and he knew his mother had left the marriage with nothing, that it was his stepfather who had supported the family all these years. Julian reported he knew nothing about any diamonds. They had lived a comfortable life. He was, or had believed he was, the son of a banker, but they didn't live in a palace or a castle, and they weren't fabulously wealthy by any standards.

But, in the back of his mind, he dreamed he would one day find the hidden treasure and keep it for himself. It was his legacy. And he wanted to make his father's dream come true.

Julian was happy to know his real father was wealthy, and he had no qualms about going into the very lucrative family import/export business. He learned about the warehouses of goods of questionable provenance that had to be sold to the highest bidder. From his father he learned to appreciate art, not the painting itself, but the value a painting could bring. There was no shortage of masterpieces he could procure for wealthy clients—individuals, art dealers, galleries, auction houses, even museums. Anything from Italian Renaissance—Botticellis, Titians, Tintorettos—and Baroque—Vermeer, Velazquez, and Klimt—to nineteenth century—Renoirs and Van Goghs. The list was endless. Of course, the transactions were not conducted on the open market. They were done in back rooms. On the black market. There was an entire shadow world of commerce to which he, Julian

Hoffman, now had an instant entrée.

He was introduced to the dozens of families who were part of the illicit but profitable and now global network. They had been trading off the misery of Holocaust victims for decades. It was the gift that kept on giving. And, like his father, he saw nothing wrong with the basic premise of the enterprise.

His father was glad to welcome his son into the family fold, since his generation, once the pride of Germany, was aging and it was time for the sons to inherit. Julian changed his last name to Hoffman and never looked back. Herr Hoffman had never remarried. Julian found a willing *Fräulein* to warm his bed and cook his meals and bear his children. She was pretty enough to look at, but he didn't trust her. He didn't trust any woman. Women were always hiding something, and they were quick to betray. So, if he beat her occasionally, it was only to put her in her place, to keep her in line.

One day, on the way to visit his grandchildren, the elder Herr Hoffman was run over by a streetcar. Julian was devastated. He lamented the lost years with his father. And he blamed his mother—for everything.

After the funeral, Julian placed a call to his mother, the first in almost a decade, to report that her husband was dead, so she could make her marriage legitimate by marrying his stepfather. He thought he was being quite generous to legitimize his half-brother and sisters. One day he would make the bastards pay. He'd make them all pay. And he would get his due. He was determined to track down the missing diamonds.

Chapter Ten
Alexander

After dinner and an exhausting but magical tour of St. Petersburg, Alexander opened his laptop but was almost too tired to concentrate.

He reviewed the day. And the night before. He had been in bed, on top of Hallelujah, ready to take the plunge, so to speak, the next step in their relationship, and, although he detected desire in her eyes, she had stopped him. For some reason, she was hesitant, and he had to respect that. But he was patient, and he was willing to wait for her to love him.

On the highlight of their tour, their excursion to the world-class Hermitage museum, with its nearly three million priceless works of art and jewelry from the private collections of Czarist nobility, he and Hallelujah had seen splendor everywhere they looked. They'd rushed from room to room to see works by Matisse, Renoir, Van Gogh, Picasso, Titian, and Rembrandt. They couldn't possibly see every piece of art there was to see. And the real masterpieces weren't even on the walls. They were the rooms in which the paintings were housed. All the while the diamonds in the suite's safe had been on his mind. Were they still there? Had someone used their time away from the ship to steal them?

They'd been impressed with the beautifully painted

baroque palaces and gilded domed churches, the Neva River, the stately squares and monuments scattered throughout the spectacular city.

Tomorrow they would travel outside the city to visit Catherine Palace, with its beautiful blue façade, and the next day they'd see the fountains and pavilions of Peterhof. The cruise was first class, and so were the tours. He was comfortable with Hallelujah. Although he had no first-hand experience with matrimony, he actually felt married, or what he thought it might feel like to be married. Unfortunately, Hallelujah's marital experience had been a disaster. He was determined to show her another way.

"Today was lovely," Hallelujah said. "St. Petersburg is so unexpected. It's the most amazing place. I'm glad I got to see it. And we have two more nights here."

"I was thinking the same thing." *Emphasis on the nights.*

They had been on a whirlwind schedule. During the day there were fascinating and exhausting excursions, and at night they'd sampled each of the ship's gourmet specialty restaurants, listened to bands, comedians, pianists, and watched the talented ensemble of singers and dancers at the nightly extravaganza production shows. They'd had late night snacks, as well as drinks at every opportunity, and had explored almost every inch of the ship. They'd even taken a tour of the galley. He was wearing her out and hopefully wearing her down. If she was overtired, she might not overthink her situation.

There were a few more stolen kisses that heated up his blood. She'd seemed responsive, but something was holding her back. Perhaps she didn't quite trust him. Whatever her reasons, she wasn't quite ready.

"Have you had any luck in your search?" she asked, twirling a lock of her hair.

Alexander turned back and tried to focus on his computer and not the nearness of her and her alluring scent. "I've been doing some research, and I found out that a man named Franz Hoffman owned my house during the last years of the war and then sold it to a family who owned it before they sold it to me. I did some digging and found that Herr Hoffman was a high-ranking SS officer, a Sturmbannführer, during the war. Quite a nasty fellow. Was never arrested or prosecuted for his crimes. As a matter of fact, they even did a profile of him in a respectable magazine. He died a very wealthy man."

Hallelujah observed the screen over Alexander's shoulder. "How does someone start out in the military during the war and end up one of the wealthiest men in Berlin? I guess all is forgiven if you're rich."

"That's not as uncommon as you think. A lot of Nazi officers walked off with priceless paintings, jewelry, and property from Jewish families who were ripped from their homes and never returned. The Nazis viewed the belongings of Jews, and their bank accounts, as German property. I can't imagine he could have prospered as much as he did unless he was up to no good, though. I'm sure he was dirty, but he probably had some powerful friends in high places so he couldn't be touched. He met with an unfortunate accident a number of years ago—it says here he was struck by a streetcar—so he couldn't be the one after us. They published a picture taken at his funeral. According to the papers, the mourners were a veritable who's who of the Nazi regime.

"I'm going to do some more research about the family that owned the house after him. They seemed like a nice family. The husband passed away and the family couldn't afford to pay the taxes, so they needed to sell in a hurry. I got a break getting into that house and that neighborhood. But somebody who was around during the war knows about those diamonds and knows I have them. I'm not sure it's just one person. There could be an entire network of people with eyes on that house, just waiting until it was sold to get their hands on what was hidden there."

"But if that were true, why didn't they just buy the house after Herr Hoffman died?"

"They didn't have to. They, whoever *they* are, arranged to rob the house. They didn't have to go to the expense of buying it. I'm convinced someone has been waiting a long time for this."

Hallelujah wrapped her arms around her shoulders.

"Are you cold?"

"Just spooked, I guess, to think that someone is lurking around, just waiting for you. Can't you go to the police?"

"What if they're involved?"

"Then someone else in the government?"

"I don't trust them, in this case. We're talking about a lot of money, and people can easily be bribed."

"What if you had been home and not at work when they broke into your house?"

"I'd have been collateral damage. Whoever it was knows I'm in the habit of working late. They've probably been watching my house. I thought it might have been the construction crew that dug up the lockbox from under the stairwell. But they never saw me open the box."

Alexander rubbed his mouth and avoided looking at her. "The truth is, they came back and roughed me up a bit. They didn't want to kill me. They wanted to scare me. It worked."

"You never told me that!" Hallelujah exclaimed. "Look at me, Alexander." He turned to her, and she placed her palm on his face. "Don't shut me out. We're in this together. You've got to tell me everything. Did they hurt you?"

"Not much, but that's when I knew I had to run. I couldn't depend on the police to protect me." He covered her hand with his. "It's nice of you to worry."

"I do worry," she admitted. "I am worried. You said the robbery happened after you had the diamonds appraised. Most likely it was someone from the jewelry store who tipped off the thief."

"That makes sense. I'm convinced that's what triggered recent events. I need to trace the ownership of the jewelry store, track down those possible connections." His fingers continued to fly across the keys. Suddenly they stopped.

"What is it? Did you find something?"

"It may just be a coincidence, but the jewelry store where I took the diamonds to be appraised was once owned by Julian Hirschfeld, before the war."

"I don't believe in coincidences," Hallelujah said. "I think this merits further investigation."

"I'm already on it," Alexander said, continuing to tap away at his keyboard.

Chapter Eleven
Julian Hoffman

"Are you sure you have the name correct? Alexander Stone? And he was the man who brought in the diamonds to be appraised?"

"Absolutely sure. I've never seen diamonds like this in my life. They were large and flawless and brilliantly cut by a master diamond cutter. As a matter of fact, I recognize the mark. It's a Hirschfeld cut. There have been diamond cutters in his family for generations. He had a royal warrant from the Queen of England. She favored his designs."

"What does that mean?"

"It's the mark of quality. These diamonds are worth a fortune. I'm positive these are the diamonds your father was looking for. They're very distinctive. Your father told my father to call him if any Hirschfeld diamonds ever surfaced or came into the store. Hirschfeld used to own this shop. He sold it under duress to my father, a casualty of war."

"Did he say where he'd found them?"

"He's the new owner of a house in the neighborhood, the house your father used to own in Dahlem. He was doing some remodeling when construction workers unearthed it. He was shocked and wanted to know their value. I think I was more shocked than he, when I saw them. We're just lucky he brought them into my shop."

"What did you tell him?"

"That they were priceless."

"Well, who is this Stone fellow?"

"Says he's some kind of hedge fund manager in Berlin. I gave him an appraisal, and he took them back. I can give you his address."

Julian wrote down the address, and thanked his friend, but he already knew the address. It was his father's old address. The house he should have been raised in. The house he would have inherited if his father hadn't given up on the diamonds and sold it in favor of a more elegant lifestyle.

He picked up the phone and issued an order.

"Yes, I want you to break in. I'll make it worth your while. Don't worry about the police. I have that covered. Break down the door with a battering ram if you have to. I need those diamonds before he moves them."

He listened and then said, "Try to break in when he's at work. But if he's there, get rid of him. Do whatever you want. I don't care. Just get me the diamonds."

****

The next day, Julian had paced his office like a caged tiger. "What do you mean they're not there?"

"We broke in while he was at work, like you said. We tore the place apart. There were no diamonds there."

"If I find out you're lying…" Julian put the threat out there.

"I had my best men on it. We left no stone unturned. There are no diamonds in that house. We even went back the next day, even though he had filed a police report. We roughed him up a little, held him at gunpoint. I even put a bullet in the wall. The kid was scared out of his mind. He said the diamonds were in a safe deposit in his bank. He was telling the truth."

"Did you bring him to the bank?"

"No, the situation was too hot. The police had just been there. He told us to meet him at his office the next morning. We left and waited for him at his office, but he never showed up to work. I called the office and his secretary said he had flown to Rome to deliver a speech and then he was taking a personal holiday. I met him at the airport. He hooked up with a woman, and they left together on a motorcycle. I tried to shoot at them, but Stone stole my gun and they got away."

"You lost them?"

"Herr Hoffman, I did the best I could."

"Not good enough. I want you to track them down. You have his name. Find out where they went, and bring back those diamonds. He must have them on him. Kill him if you have to. Just get those diamonds."

"What about the woman? Do you want me to hurt her?"

"What do I care about the woman? If he won't talk, make her talk. Or bring them to me. I'll make them talk."

Chapter Twelve
Hallelujah and Alexander

AS THE PLANET SPINS SCRIPT EXTRACT
BY HALLELUJAH WEISS
SCENE 4.
THE LIVING ROOM OF THE WINTRHOP ESTATE.
PARKER: Polly, I want to start again.
POLLY: You want a do-over?
PARKER: Exactly. Like the time you slept with Lance behind my back and I forgave you.
POLLY: I had amnesia. When I woke up from my coma, I thought Lance and I were still married.
PARKER: Why do we keep hurting each other?
POLLY: I wish I knew the answer to that question.
PARKER: I've turned over a new leaf. I promise I won't cheat.
POLLY: Don't make promises you can't keep.
PARKER: You have to trust me.
POLLY: No, that's the thing, Parker, I don't trust you.
PARKER: But you love me.
POLLY: I wish those feelings weren't mutually exclusive.
PARKER: [GRABS POLLY AND KISSES HER] Remember what it felt like when we were happy? We were happy together, Polly.
POLLY: [BREATHLESS] I can't stop remembering. I keep thinking—

PARKER: Stop thinking and kiss me, Pollyanna.
****

Hallelujah woke from a deep, drugging sleep, warm and…happy, and tingly, down to her toes. The European down comforter was cozy. She didn't want to leave the bed, but a rosy light streamed laser-like through the picture window. She'd overslept. Her eyes rose to the mirror on the ceiling.

Correction. *They'd* overslept.

Alexander was wrapped around her like an octopus. He was snoring slightly, and as she moved, he tightened his grip on her. She didn't know what she thought about that. Had they slept together last night? Hopefully not in the biblical sense. They'd both had too much champagne, but she would have remembered that. He had given her a chaste kiss on the lips in the circular bed, and that's the last thing she remembered. But now, and there was the evidence right there on the ceiling, they were tangled together, arms and legs intertwined. Apparently, they had turned to each other in the middle of the night and found the position comfortable. Chalk it up to gravitational pull—or the rocking motion of the ship—that had brought them together.

"Alexander," she whispered loudly. "Alexander, are you awake?"

He issued a muffled sound. His mouth was up against her lips, and he shifted and kissed her. She could feel his erection. Apparently he went from zero to sixty on the arousal meter in about two seconds. She had been wearing a sheer negligee, and it was slightly off her shoulder. One breast was exposed, and when his mouth latched on to her nipple, still half asleep, she shivered.

"Alexander, get off me. I can't breathe." She tried to shift away from his body but found herself trapped in the circular bed with a naked man she hardly knew. Well, they were married, but still...

His mouth moved back to her lips, and she felt him smile, but he didn't loosen his grip.

"I'm pretty comfortable at the moment."

"I feel like I'm wrapped in a cocoon. I can't move."

He kissed her again gently on the lips and whispered, "I've got you just where I want you."

"Alexander Stone, you must be hung over."

"Just hung up, on you."

His erection stiffened against her. He definitely had hanky-panky on his mind. He slipped the negligee off her shoulder, exposing her other breast, and kissed her nipple. It tightened, betraying her.

"I think you liked that."

"I don't think you're fully awake, and you're naked. So I'll overlook your behavior. We're going to miss our excursion."

"It's a sea day."

"Oh."

"Hallelujah, admit it. You want me as much as I want you."

She tried to shift away from his grasp, but her movement only seemed to arouse him further.

"Maybe I'm dreaming, but I don't want to wake up." He rose above her and slipped off her panties. He kissed her again. She looked up at the mirror.

"Alexander, I feel like I woke up in a porno film. I went to bed in a nightgown and now I'm completely nude, and you're—I mean, look at us."

"I don't want to look up. I'm looking at you, and I'm going to tell you exactly what I want to do with you."

He grasped her hands and pushed them above her head so she was pinned on the bed. He teased her with his body. Then he kissed each nipple and took her lips.

She groaned. "Alexander, this isn't like you."

"I'm tired of being Mr. Nice Guy, Boring Hedge Fund Manager." She squirmed, but that just excited him more.

"Do you really want me to stop?"

She had to admit her body didn't want him to stop, but who knew about her mind? Whatever he was doing to her down there felt good, really good, but she had to put the brakes on before she regretted it.

"Oh, God," she moaned.

"Is that a yes or a no?" He kept up the torture.

"We're not ready."

"We, as in you and me? Or we, as in you and Polly? Because I know I'm ready."

She gathered her strength, loosened his grip on her hands, and flipped him so she was on top.

Alexander's eyebrows rose in surprise and expectation. "If you want to take the lead, I can handle that."

"Lloyd blamed Parker for our breakup. He said he could never measure up to Parker's standards."

"There are too many people in this bed, Hallelujah. I don't want to talk about Lloyd or Parker or Polly, just you and me."

"I just don't want to make the same mistake."

Alexander blew out a breath.

"Message received," sighed Alexander, pulling away. "I'm going to take a cold shower. For God's sake, get dressed then, Hallelujah."

"What does God have to do with this?"

Alexander shook his head. "You're the rabbi's daughter. You tell me." Alexander rolled off the bed and padded into the bathroom.

Hallelujah had to empty her bladder, but she wasn't going to do it in front of him. The marriage was on paper only. So she would hold it in until he came out of the shower.

She took her laptop and sat outside their cabin on a deck chair, watching lights go on in the houses that dotted the picturesque islands as they sailed toward Stockholm, dreaming up dialogue for Parker and Polly, but mostly daydreaming about Alexander.

Chapter Thirteen
Julian Hoffman

"I hope you have good news for me." Julian got a stranglehold on his cell phone. He'd been expecting this call for days.

"I've found them, Herr Hoffman."

Julian stopped pacing.

"Well?" Julian said impatiently.

"They're on a cruise."

"A cruise?"

"A Scandinavian cruise."

"What?"

"A Scandinavian cruise. They're not even using fake passports. We put in Stone's name and it came up. They've been sailing on the Baltic all this time."

Julian cursed.

"And another thing. He's gotten married."

"Married?"

"To that woman he was with at the airport in Rome. Her name is Hallelujah Evans Weiss—well, now it's Hallelujah Stone."

"What kind of name is that?"

"She's Jewish."

Julian tightened the grip on his cell phone.

"When do they dock? And where?"

"In Stockholm, two days from now."

"You will have people waiting to greet the

newlyweds when they disembark."

"We will?"

"Are you dense? Of course you will. Have we not been chasing this pair around Europe? And now we've caught the lovebirds in our snare. You will be waiting. I suggest a driver holding a sign with their names when they come into baggage claim. With a complimentary ride to their destination. It will be our wedding present."

"What is their destination, Herr Hoffman?"

"That is up to you to find out, you idiot. Don't disappoint me again."

"And where will I take them?"

"Straight back to Berlin, of course. To me. To the warehouse, where we'll be undisturbed."

"But what if they won't come with me?"

"I trust you will find a way, *any* way, even if you have to drug them. Just deliver the lovebirds to me. And I will cage them and make them sing."

Julian powered down his cell phone and sat at his desk until his heart stopped hammering.

Finally, things were coming together. He put his feet on the desk and contemplated his situation. It's not that he didn't have enough money. The *Gruppen* was so flush they couldn't spend the profits they had in a lifetime. He had the Midas Touch. His father had even said so. Of course, when you start out with billions, it's easy to make more. The war had been over for decades, yet people were always in the market for valuable artwork and priceless jewelry. He hadn't been around when it was liquidated, so to speak, so his hands were clean. He certainly hadn't killed anyone, *yet*.

Julian looked at his nails. *Remind self to make an*

appointment for a sports manicure.

His father and his father's contemporaries had accumulated the goods, which at the time might or might not have been misappropriated. But if his father had taught him anything, it was that money was fungible. It was neither good nor bad. Money was money, and there was hardly anyone around who remembered the war. No one to accuse the corporation. By now, goods had been sold and resold so many times the origins had grown hazy. Some of the more valuable works of art had been stored for decades, and so many years had passed, the provenances were practically nonexistent.

Case in point. He was about to deliver a Rembrandt to one of the top auction houses in Europe. The masterpiece was very much in demand. No one knew where it had come from, and no one would know how it got there. And no one wanted to know. But there was no doubt that it would fetch a fortune. And part of that fortune would go to him in the form of a hefty fee. There were warehouses full of such pieces, pieces the world believed were lost forever. Knowing when and where to let them surface was an art in itself, an art he had perfected.

It was really very easy. Oh, occasionally a relative would surface and demand restitution for a painting that had been in the family for generations. But that wasn't his problem. His involvement was not traceable. These cases, if they went to court at all, were rarely won. Could rarely be proven. And if they happened to get a favorable ruling, the complainant was often dead before the case had been litigated.

Since his father died, he had been put in charge of

Zersetzung Gruppen KG. And he had doubled the assets of the enterprise. Maybe some of his stepfather's banking skills had rubbed off on him.

If only his mother could see him now. She thought he was a failure. And it was true, he was rudderless before he rediscovered his roots. His life had been meaningless. And that was her fault. She had never loved him. Oh, she would think the whole endeavor was corrupt, evil. But it was just business. No doubt his father had cashed in on some of her family's possessions. And rightfully so. She was his property. She belonged to him. And then she left—stole his son and walked away. He could never forgive her for that. And he, Julian, was finally going to get revenge. He would get the diamonds from Herr Stone, who would talk, or be tortured, or watch while his new wife was tortured. Julian would have some fun with her, even if she was a Jew. His wife was beginning to bore him. And then, when he recovered the diamonds, he was going to go back to Switzerland and make his mother pay for all those wasted, lonely years.

Chapter Fourteen
Hallelujah and Alexander

Hallelujah was sorry to see the cruise come to an end. There would be one last City of Stockholm excursion, and then they would board a flight to Switzerland. It had been a relaxing week, even though Alexander must have checked his package in the safe a million times and, every time, was relieved to learn that the diamonds were still there. He'd initially been nervous, envisioning that people were after him wherever they went, but as the journey progressed, he relaxed, and he'd been a wonderful companion. Very engaging, willing to try anything, going out of his way to make her happy. He let her pick the excursions, the restaurants, everything except for the surprise steak dinner on their "wedding night." He insisted on buying her lavish gifts at the ship's boutiques, saying he enjoyed having someone special to spend his money on. They went dancing every night, and she felt cherished in his arms.

They hadn't talked about what would happen after the ship docked, except she'd agreed to go to Switzerland with him to talk to Eva Grandcoeur. In fact, she was looking forward to meeting Eva. Maybe Eva's story was the one she was looking for. But after that, she intended to go to Florence and resume the new life she'd planned for her "Get Over Lloyd" junket.

In truth, Lloyd wasn't much on her mind anymore. Her anger toward Lloyd and her resentment of Olivia had dissipated into the ocean. There was another man who now occupied her attention. She would miss Alexander. But "All Good Things Must Come to an End." It was just like life on her soap. People never stayed happy for long. There was always some disaster lurking around the corner. Alexander would be going back to resume his life and career in Berlin, and that was the absolute last place on earth she wanted to live. Or even visit.

She had her work, which was very fulfilling, and hopefully would have plenty of Lloyd's money. She made enough of her own that using his money wasn't even necessary. She could support herself. Did Lloyd even miss the Monet yet? Let him stew for a while. RaeLynn had it safely hidden away in a temperature-controlled storage locker, with strict instructions not to take any of Lloyd's calls. And if he called her about the painting, she'd laugh it off and say she must have accidentally thrown it out. Olivia fancied herself an amateur artist. Maybe she could paint him another one. Ha, ha. She'd seen Olivia's drawings. Not likely.

She watched Alexander as his fingers flew across the keyboard. He thought of himself as nerdy, had confided that girls found him boring. She found him fascinating. He was smart and sensitive and surprisingly normal. And more than that, she found him sexy. Very sexy. In fact, she wanted to sneak up behind him and slide her fingers lightly along his neck, massage his shoulders, and...

"Hallelujah!" he exclaimed, turning abruptly. "What are you doing?" His outburst didn't sound like a complaint. It was more like the tone you used when you'd just won the lottery.

She was doing it again. Without realizing it, she had stepped out of her daydreams and translated her desires to action. A hazard of being a soap opera scribe and a drama queen.

He grabbed her and yanked her down onto his lap, wedging her between his body and the computer. Then he began kissing her, urgently. He filled his hands with her breasts. Suddenly, she found herself sitting on top of a giant boner. Mount Vesuvius was about to blow. And she was erupting, too…emotionally, that is.

"Alexander," she sighed. She knew she was being naughty and giving in to her desires just to satisfy herself. Just like Polly. She never wanted him to stop kissing her and touching her. But was she leading him on? He had genuine feelings for her. But they were totally wrong for each other. Her parents would never understand. But maybe just this once…

"God," she said, bursting with desire as Alexander began grinding himself against her crotch.

"Let's move to the bed, where we'll be more comfortable," he said, lifting her and placing her gently on the mattress.

Then there was nothing gentle about it. They tore at each other. She was eager to shed her clothes, and he was eager to help her do it. He kissed her until her lips were swollen, and then first his tongue and then his mouth moistened her nipples. His teeth were taking a bite— Suddenly she was naked and so was he, and he was touching her everywhere and trying to enter her. And she was howling. Or was that a seagull?

"Don't stop," she pleaded.

"I couldn't if I wanted to."

And then a door buzzer sounded. "Housekeeping."

"Go away!" Alexander shouted in every language he could think of.

And then the hordes came barreling down the hall just as the captain's voice came over the intercom, interrupting the much anticipated eruption.

"We're about to arrive in Stockholm."

"Fuck Stockholm," Alexander ranted.

Then Hallelujah made the mistake of looking up at that damn mirror.

"This is crazy," she lamented.

"Dammit, no, it's not," he insisted, as they heard the key unlock the door.

Hallelujah dove under the covers just as Alexander shouted out, "Come back later. We're on our honeymoon."

The housekeeper looked at the two of them in bed. Alexander was naked as a jaybird, and Hallelujah looked up at the mirror, which just made it worse, because everyone knew that *objects appear larger than they really are,* and the housekeeper apologized and backed out of the cabin.

"Hallelujah?" he inquired, trying to locate her under the sheets.

"Go away."

"It's okay," he said. "She's gone. They're gone. They're all gone." He looked down at himself. "Well, not everything is gone."

"It's not okay. It's too late. This is not going to work."

"I thought you wanted— What do you mean? This, here, now? Or us?"

Hallelujah wrapped the sheet around her body and walked into the bathroom.

"Us, this, whatever. It's never going to work."

"Do you want to talk about it?"

"No," she said, pursing her lips, tears staining her eyes. "And don't come in after me."

How could she explain she was crazy in love with this man she hardly knew, was dying for him to be inside of her, but it definitely was Not. Going. To. Work. For too many reasons to count.

Chapter Fifteen
Hallelujah and Alexander

AS THE PLANET SPINS SCRIPT EXTRACT
BY HALLELUJAH WEISS
SCENE 5. FLORENCE AIRPORT, PERETOLA.
POLLY: [UPBEAT] It's great to be back in Florence.
PARKER: The place where we first fell in love. Il Duomo, the Uffizi Gallery, the Piazza della Signoria, the Ponte Vecchio, and you.
POLLY: And don't forget the stracciatella gelato. I remember. Florence is so romantic. I hope we can recapture the love we felt for each other.
PARKER: The love I still feel for you, Pollyanna.
POLLY: How many times did you save me, Parker? There was the incident with the grizzly bear on our first honeymoon in the Canadian Rockies. And the time those Somali pirates boarded our yacht in the Mediterranean. I really thought that was the end. And the time we were kidnapped outside our hotel by those Middle Eastern terrorists.
PARKER: But you have the courage to save yourself. Remember the time you were kidnapped by those South American drug lords? I was so frantic, but you managed to untie yourself, steal their mobile phone, and dial 1-1-2.
POLLY: How could I forget? I'll never know how I remembered that emergency number.

PARKER: We make a good team.
****

Hallelujah and Alexander walked into the Stockholm Airport with their bags. Hallelujah scanned the terminal.

"Alexander, look. There's a sign with our name on it."

"I didn't order a driver. The plan was we were going to take a plane to Zurich directly from here, and then a train to Baden."

"Maybe it's part of our wedding package," Hallelujah suggested.

"It's not. Don't look at him. That driver has no idea who we are. Let's keep it that way. No one is supposed to know we're here."

"Do you really think we're being followed?"

"He must have followed us from the ship. I just want to stick to the plan. Things usually work out better that way."

Hallelujah pouted. It was actually the classic Polly pout, the pout of someone who came from a long line of non-planners. "What's wrong with a ride in a limousine?"

Alexander turned her face away from the chauffeur. "Let's just head for security."

The chauffeur's eyes fell on Alexander. He walked over and held up his poster board.

"Herr Stone. I'm here to pick up you and your lovely bride."

Alexander stiffened. "I think there's been some mistake."

"Are you not the Stones?"

"I'm afraid you have the wrong couple." Alexander

grabbed Hallelujah's hand and started running toward security.

"Grab your bags and go. Just ignore him. He's speaking German. He's not some Swedish driver. He's followed us from Berlin. Follow me and get in line behind me."

Hallelujah ran after Alexander, but someone was pulling her back. She turned around. It was the driver. She kicked him and brought her purse down on his head. He stumbled, and she kept running toward security.

"Wait," he called. She heard footsteps. He was closing in fast.

Alexander turned around and grabbed her hand.

They passed a security guard and Hallelujah yelled, "That man behind me—he has a bomb."

Suddenly all hell broke loose. Bomb-sniffing dogs and security officers surrounded the man with the sign and dragged him away. Guns were drawn, and people scattered and screamed. Alexander and Hallelujah continued calmly toward the security line.

"Quick thinking. He's not going to be a problem."

"Polly did the same thing at an airport in London when she was trying to get away from the paparazzi."

Alexander shook his head. "Is there anything Polly hasn't done?"

"We've been on the air for years, so no, not really. You know they're going to release that man once they discover he doesn't have a bomb. And he knows we're getting on another flight."

"But we could be going anywhere in the world."

"True. Finding us will be like finding a needle in a haystack."

"If he ever gets out of customs, he can track us," Alexander pointed out. "We're using our real names and passports. But, hopefully, we can make it to Zurich and to the train station before he figures it out. He can't be working alone. Sooner or later, they're going to find us. I hope Polly has some other tricks up her sleeve."

Chapter Sixteen
Eva Grandcouer

Baden, Switzerland, Present Day

The nurse helped the old woman from her prone position and propped her up against her feather pillows. She informed her patient that there were two visitors, a young couple, and despite her years, and the fact that she didn't know these people, she was fastidious and wanted to maintain a good appearance. The nurse ran a comb through the woman's hair and freshened her lipstick.

Alexander and Hallelujah walked into the room. He extended his hand. "Eva Grandcoeur?"

The woman nodded, placed a wrinkled hand in his, and then released it.

The man came close to her bed to address her.

"I am Alexander Stone. And this is my friend Hallelujah Weiss."

The old woman pursed her lips. Hallelujah came out from the shadows and smiled tentatively. *Alexander hadn't said wife. Now that the cruise was over, she was reduced to a friend.* The woman's eyes founds hers.

"Weiss. You are a Jew?"

Hallelujah nodded. The woman expelled a calming breath.

"Thank you for seeing us. We've come a long way

to ask you some questions, if you don't mind. Do you know a family called the Hirschfelds? Father Julian, Mother Ana, daughter Hannah, and young son Aaron."

Eva's smile never quite made it to her face. *Hannah Hirschfeld.* It had been many years since she'd heard that name.

"Why do you ask?"

"Because there were four stumble stones placed outside my house in Dahlem to commemorate that family. I live in the house now, their house, the house where the Hirschfeld family lived before the war."

"Your house?"

"Yes, I recently bought it."

"How did you find me?"

"Your name was on a receipt. You paid for four stumble stones in that family's name. Did you know them?"

The woman kneaded her hands together, considered her answer for a minute or two, and finally said, "Yes."

"Do you remember what happened to the family?" Alexander asked.

The woman closed her eyes and grimaced before she looked up at Alexander. "I was there the day they were rounded up."

She placed her hand over her eyes and bowed her head, as though searching her memory. She seemed to struggle for a breath.

"What do you remember about that day?" Alexander asked.

"I remember hiding in the space under the stairs," said Eva clearly. "I heard footsteps, and a pounding noise at the front door. I was so frightened, but I stayed where I was, following my mother's instructions. I heard the argument between one of the officers, a Sturmbannführer, and my father. I will never forget his voice as long as I live. He had my parents and little brother dragged away to the camps. For the next hour, footsteps were everywhere on the hardwood floors, on the Aubussons. I heard furniture being turned over, boxes opened. I froze there in my hiding place. When the noises were gone, I walked out into the living room. Drawers were opened, our possessions were strewn everywhere. I wanted my mother, but she was gone. Then the neighbor from next door, a friend of my mother's, a fine Catholic woman, opened the door.

" 'Hannah, are you in here?' She found me and told me she had seen my mother being taken away. I was to go with her, the neighbor; she was to care for me until my mother returned. But of course she never returned. I looked around and saw a family picture on the floor. The glass was broken, but I removed the picture and took her hand. She hid me in her house for the remainder of the war. I didn't go to school. I didn't go outside at all."

"Like Anne Frank," whispered Hallelujah. "But luckier."

The woman shook her head. "Maybe not so lucky. To this day, I still crave the sunlight. Our villa in Dahlem was open to the sun, skylights everywhere. While I was in hiding, I was always in the dark. When the war was over, my guardian helped me look for my parents, but they were gone, along with the rest of my family. My mother's friend raised me as her own. She called me Eva. I still have that picture."

Hannah pointed to a black-and-white picture in a

frame, surrounded by a cotillion of more recent color family pictures. "There, that's me."

Alexander was struck by Hannah's appearance. She must have been a beauty in her day.

"You're Hannah?"

"Yes, I was Hannah Hirschfeld."

Alexander was stunned. He looked at Hallelujah.

"What happened to you after the war?" Hallelujah asked gently.

Hannah sat up straight and adjusted her pillow. "I grew up, met a man, had children of my own, and grandchildren. I—" The way she hesitated, Hallelujah could tell there was more to the story.

"If you're Hannah, then I have something for you, something of your father's that belongs to you." Alexander handed Hannah the pouch of diamonds, yellowing travel papers—proof of permission to leave Germany, certificates of good conduct from German police authorities, and other identity papers required to apply for entry visas to emigrate to another country—and a stack of family pictures. She examined the contents of the bag. She ignored the diamonds and the faded travel papers and, instead, flipped through the family pictures. Her eyes teared up. She began to shake.

"We've upset her," Hallelujah whispered to Alexander.

"It's fine. It's just been so long." She sighed.

"Hannah, the diamonds. They belonged to your family. I found them in your house when I was doing some renovations, and I'm bringing them to you."

"Diamonds? What would I want with these? They did my father no good. They got my family murdered."

"They are your heritage," Alexander said.

"What am I going to do with them now? I'm an old lady. I'm at the end of my life."

"Perhaps for your children or grandchildren?" Alexander reasoned.

"What do I need with diamonds? Years ago, maybe, they might have meant something. These transit papers might have meant something, if my father had handed over the diamonds to Herr Hoffman. And with a few exceptions, there are no survivors left to share the proceeds. But wealth is highly overrated."

"It must cost a lot to live here," Alexander pointed out. "For your care."

"I won't be staying very long."

"How do we know what God has in store for us?" Hallelujah interjected, lifting Hannah's frail hand. Always the rabbi's daughter, she echoed the words of her father and tried to provide comfort for this woman, with whom she felt a strong connection.

Hannah laughed, a low-throated warble. "You're still very young—Hallelujah, is it? You haven't had a chance to be disappointed. I will take the pictures, though. They are the only things that have any meaning for me."

Alexander pressed the photos, tied in a bundle with a blue ribbon, into the woman's hand.

"Mrs. Grandcoeur, you're not thinking straight. I came a long way to find out what happened to the family and return what is rightfully theirs. What is now rightfully yours."

"Well, then, I'm afraid you've wasted your time," Hannah answered coolly.

Alexander shook his head.

Then the woman picked up one of the diamonds

and smiled.

"My father made jewelry for the Queen of England, did you know? This is the Hirschfeld mark. The mark of my family. He came from a long line of jewelers. It was a source of pride. He always said that one day he would design my engagement ring. 'If it was good enough for a queen, it's good enough for my princess.' That's what my father used to call me."

She wiped a tear away and put the diamond back in the pile. "I see I've disappointed you. Well, that's because you don't know the whole story."

"I'd like to hear it." Alexander slipped into a padded wing chair across from Eva. Hallelujah sat on the woman's bed and continued to hold her hand. She could read people, and her instincts told her this woman needed her to stay close by.

"I learned much of the story after the war," Eva began. "There were some survivors. The diamonds weren't my father's alone to trade. You see, all of his friends got together and liquidated their assets and brought my father money, which he used to buy diamonds to negotiate safe passage for themselves and their families. He also held the travel papers, without which the families could not escape. So my father didn't jeopardize just his family but all those families who had entrusted their lives to him. When he planned to head out early that day, he was not only signing our death warrant but the death warrants of all of the families who had trusted him. It was a monstrous betrayal. I had to make it right, so I did what I had to do, no matter the cost. Where did you find the diamonds?"

"I was remodeling the area around the bottom of

the staircase, and the construction crew found the lockbox. It was filled with the diamonds and the travel visas and the family photos."

"Under the staircase?" Eva's hands flew to her throat. "That's where I was hiding that day, the day that monster came to our house."

"Mrs. Grandcoeur, it is obvious your father didn't betray anyone. He couldn't give up the diamonds because he would have given away your hiding place."

Tears streamed down Eva's face at the truth of Alexander's words. Her father had saved her life. All those years... She had wasted all those years hating her father.

"And knowing what we now know of the Nazi character, the Sturmbannführer would certainly have taken the diamonds and deported your family anyway," reasoned Alexander. "Your father made the only decision he could have. A decision any father would have made."

"Do you have children, Mr. Stone?"

Alexander glanced at Hallelujah. "Not yet. But I hope to, one day soon."

Eva tightened her grip on Hallelujah's hand. "Do you know Hebrew?"

"Yes," Hallelujah said, adding, "My father is a rabbi."

"A rabbi. Well, then, do you know the Mourner's Kaddish?"

Hallelujah nodded. "Of course."

"Would you say it for me, for my parents and my baby brother? After the war, I hid the fact that I was Jewish. It's very dangerous to be a Jew in this world, you see. I've never acknowledged my religion. I don't believe the Germans will ever truly confront their past, and I don't believe they want to."

"I think you're right," Hallelujah agreed. "Once when my father went on a trip to the Dachau concentration camp, he got lost and stopped a townsperson to get directions. The man said he never heard of Dachau. My father thought perhaps it was a miscommunication, that the man didn't understand English, so my father prompted, *"Konzentrationslage, KZ,"* and the man still looked puzzled and said he never heard of that place. Right beyond him, only inches away, was a sign for the camp. I have to believe they are still ashamed of it and don't want visitors to see. When he got there, at the end of the tour were the ovens. And there was a survivor who said he came every day to talk to visitors about the Holocaust so people would never forget and would know it really happened. My father's account of that visit, and of the man's personal history, has always stayed with me. The number of Holocaust survivors continues to drop. I doubt that he is even still there."

Hallelujah cleared her throat and began to recite the prayer. *"Yitgadal veyitkadash shmei raba, bealma divera chireutei veyamlich malchutei, bechayeichon uveyomeichon uvechayei dechol beit Yisrael, baagala uvizeman kariv, veyimeru…"*

"Amen," chanted Eva and Hallelujah, in unison.

Hallelujah recited the remainder of the prayer for the dead without a hitch, without hesitation.

"Now I can die in peace," whispered Eva, as the women embraced and Alexander watched.

A nurse came in with a lunch tray for Eva. Hallelujah offered to feed her and dismissed the nurse.

"Did you ever return to your parents' house?" Hallelujah asked after Eva finished eating.

Eva nodded. "Yes, I—"

"And what ever happened to the Sturmbannführer who had your family deported?" Hallelujah interrupted.

Eva smiled. "I married him and moved back into my house. We had a son together."

Hallelujah couldn't hide her shock, and for once, she was speechless.

"She asks a lot of questions," Alexander explained.

"I'd be happy to give you all the answers. It's a long story."

"We're not going anywhere," Alexander said.

For the next hour, Alexander and Hallelujah listened as Eva recounted the events of her life during and after the war. When she was done talking, she yawned. "I'm feeling a little tired now. I'd like to rest for a while."

"Of course," Hallelujah said. "We've worn you out. I'm sorry. But I have to know. Did you ever return to Germany after you ran away?"

"No, I never went back there after I came to Switzerland. Too many bad memories. I later learned that Herr Hoffman was hit by a trolley car in Berlin. So maybe there is justice in the world."

"Did he ever find out what happened to you?" Alexander asked.

"Not at the time. I just left, like a thief in the middle of the night, without an explanation, pregnant with his child. I hope I caused him a lot of sleepless nights."

"Does your son know who his father was?"

"He thought his father was Hans-Peter Grandcoeur.

But one day he learned the truth, and I never saw him again. He called when his real father died, anxious to tell me that he was following in his father's footsteps."

Eva's eyelashes fluttered, and she drifted off to sleep. Hallelujah and Alexander stayed by her bedside.

"That is an amazing story," Hallelujah said. "I have to write it. People have to know. I'll ask Eva's permission when she wakes up."

About an hour later, Eva sat up in bed. She seemed alert and refreshed and eager to continue their conversation.

"There's something that's been bothering me," said Alexander. "I've spent months trying to find a relative of the Hirschfelds. But according to the stumble stone in front of my house, you died in Auschwitz with the rest of your family."

"Did you know that some one point one million people were murdered in Auschwitz?" Eva said, lowering her voice. "Few survived. But when I heard about the artist's memorial project, I arranged to fund the *stolpersteine* for my family, and the ceremony. I added a stone for myself because, in my mind, Hannah Hirschfeld died that day. I should have been with my family. I should have died with them."

Alexander picked up the family portrait on the side table. "Then what would have happened to your wonderful children?"

Tears slipped out of Eva's eyes.

"Hannah, Eva, what am I to do with these diamonds?"

"Whatever you want."

"I have an idea," Hallelujah suggested. "Why don't we gift the proceeds of their sale to the Stumble Stones project, and your diamonds will fund even more commemorative plaques. We could donate the money in the name of the Hirschfeld family. That would be your legacy."

"That's a great idea." Alexander turned to Eva. "What would you think of that?"

Eva's mouth formed a hint of a smile. "I think that's a wonderful idea. But it must be in the name of Hannah Hirschfeld. For the first time in a long time, I'm proud of that name. Mr. Stone, Alexander, let me call my son Aaron. I named him after my little brother. I like to think that Aaron would have grown up to look just like my son. I'll have him bring over the documents I collected in Berlin."

"What documents?" Alexander inquired.

After making the brief telephone call to her son, she continued. "I have a complete record of all the transactions and corruption my former husband and his friends were involved in—names, dates, places. Some of the biggest corporations in the country are involved in this scandal. I'd like you to take it to the authorities, and if you don't get any cooperation, then I want you to send it to the newspapers."

"How did you get this information?" Alexander asked.

"I was their unofficial stenographer. After the war, I got a job as a typist in an accounting office. Franz made me quit working after we were married, but I was a good typist, and I typed up all the transactions for his corporation. The names of the paintings they stole, who they belonged to, where the paintings were sold, how much they were sold for, and who they were sold to. I recognized many of the works of art. Some were from my own home."

"You truly have a complete record of all of these stolen goods?"

"Yes, artwork, jewelry, deeds to houses…"

Hallelujah held Eva's hand. "Do you realize what this could mean? If we could trace the provenance of a painting, for example, it could be returned to its rightful owner. Restitution could be made to the victims or their heirs."

"But so many years have passed."

"Yes, but if you have proof of the original ownership of these goods, even if the paintings changed hands several times, they can be traced, used in court cases. It would shave years off a search." She turned to Alexander.

"Hallelujah is absolutely right. I know just the firm who could handle it."

"When I married Herr Hoffman, I just wanted revenge. Now I want justice. Do you really think my notes could make a difference?"

"Absolutely. You would probably have to be deposed. With some help, I'm going to break this conglomerate wide open."

"But this enterprise group, *Zersetzung Gruppen KG*, is so powerful. I read about them every day in the papers here."

"They don't own everyone or everything," Alexander stated.

This outcome was more than Alexander could have hoped for. If the corrupt conglomerate or executives were exposed, he and Hallelujah would not have to hide forever. For surely they were involved in the break-in at his house, and the threats.

"Back then, they secretly referred to themselves as the *Unternehmen Gruppen* or U-Group for short," said Eva.

"Why is that?" asked Alexander.

"Because that name was reminiscent of the U-boats that did so much damage to the Allies during the war. They thought that was clever. Only they were hidden underground, not undersea. They got prosperous profiting off other people's misery. The names I have gathered date back to the war. By now the organization no doubt has tentacles that reach into the higher echelons of German commerce. You'll have to follow the money trail to see where it leads, no matter where it leads. Do I have your promise?"

"Yes," Alexander stated. "I will get justice for you and for your family. I'm familiar with this firm. As a matter of fact, at one time they did a transaction with my firm. They were a bit on the shady side, with a seemingly bottomless pit of cash. And now I know where it comes from."

The nurse appeared at the door. "Mrs. Grandcoeur, you have another visitor. Your son Aaron is here."

Aaron's eyes lit up when he saw his mother. Hannah's love for her son was reflected in her own eyes.

"Aaron, I'd like you to meet my new friends. Alexander Stone and Hallelujah Weiss, this is my son Aaron."

Aaron shook Alexander's hand and smiled at Hallelujah.

"Did you bring the files?"

"Yes, Mother. Everything is right here."

"Please give them to Mr. Stone. He will make sure

they go to the right place."

Aaron handed over a large briefcase to Alexander.

"My mother has held on to these for a long time. She never told me what was in this briefcase, only that I should guard it with my life."

"Son, I will tell you the whole story, but now my friends have a big job to do."

Alexander lifted some of the files out of the briefcase.

"I'm afraid some of the papers may have yellowed with age," Eva said.

"But they're still legible," Alexander asserted.

He sat down and reviewed the information in the files. His finger paused at one listing.

"This name is familiar, Abraham Hammerman. An Abraham Hammerman is one of the founding partners and former CEO and Chairman of my hedge fund firm in Berlin, Hammerman GmbH. He still serves on the supervisory board, but his son has taken over his position. Mr. Hammerman was my mentor. I know him very well."

Hannah shook her head. "No, that is not possible. His wife Madeline was my mother's best friend. But you say you know this man? It can't be the same person. Abraham Hammerman was killed during the war."

"Did he live in Dahlem?"

"Yes, I saw Mr. Hammerman's wife after the war. She was the one who told me my parents and brother were dead. Hers was a sad story. When she was taken, she had just found out she was pregnant. She hadn't even told her husband. They were separated when they arrived on the train at the camp. He went one way, she another. They had to leave all their clothes and jewelry before they went into the showers. But of course, at that time they had no idea where they were really headed.

"There was a beautiful red wool coat Mr. Hammerman had just bought his wife," Eva continued. "She was very proud of that coat. And she had to leave that behind. Then when she was walking into the shower area, she was pulled out of line by a guard who said, "Come with me." She was confused in all of the chaos. They were all confused. But she went with the guard and later found out she had been singled out as part of a group of women to be used for the officers' pleasure. Some were sent to service the soldiers on the front. In her case, she had caught the eye of an SS officer, one very high up in the command chain, when she first came into camp. And she became his woman. At first she resisted. She refused to submit. But she didn't have a choice if she wanted to save her child. And he led her to believe she held her husband's life in her hands. Later, much later, the officer told Madeline her husband was dead.

"She said she was little more than a prostitute. She did some light cleaning and worked in the kitchen, but her living conditions were far superior to that of the average prisoners, who barely survived in cold, unsanitary, crowded barracks, who could never get enough to eat and were subject to daily pre-dawn roll calls and the cruel and capricious whims of sadistic officers.

"She felt ashamed, but she had no choice if she wanted to save the life she was carrying inside her. Later, when she told the man she was pregnant, she lied and said it was his child, and when the baby was born—

a little girl—he arranged to move the child to a farm outside the camp and paid the farmer's wife to care for her. If Madeline hadn't been protected, she would certainly have been subject to Dr. Mengele's experiments on pregnant women. And she stayed alive because one day she hoped to be reunited with her daughter. The officer promised her if she continued to please him, he would take her to her daughter. He never did."

"What happened next?" Hallelujah prompted.

"At some point the officer was promoted and transferred back to Berlin, and the new commandant established a brothel beside the main gate of the camp to provide incentives to prisoners. Typically, the women were not Jews, but in Madeline's case, since she had been the officer's woman, they made an exception. She was forced to work in the brothel. The Jewish prisoners were not sympathetic to her plight. Her officer eventually came back to Auschwitz, but by then she had become a liability to him, so she remained in the brothel until the camp was liberated in January 1945.

"She was ashamed to tell me. I knew something about shame. So I understood her dilemma. She chose life. Her Abe had gone the other way in line, the way of my father before he was shot, so naturally she thought she knew his fate. Then, after the war, she found Abraham's name on a list of victims, so she knew what the SS officer had told her about her husband being dead was true.

"She was liberated by Soviet troops and had to make her own way back home. She was happy to put as much distance as possible between herself and Max.

That was the SS officer. But she was also getting farther away from her daughter. She met an American soldier while she was at the displaced persons camp, and she enlisted his help to find her child. When they found her, she was very grateful. There was nothing for her in Berlin, so she married the American, and the three of them moved to the United States. He's passed away, but she is still living in New York."

"Did they have other children?" Hallelujah asked.

"No, she was unable to have more children because of the things that happened to her at the camp after her officer left."

"I am quite sure this is the same man," Alexander said. "I know the family. Abraham's wife Madeline was killed at Auschwitz. Or so he believed. It's the same name. Abraham and Madeline Hammerman. That can't be a coincidence. He didn't like to talk about the war, but once, many years later, he told us his name had been on the list of the dead but that he had escaped."

"How did he do that?" Eva asked. "I heard it was almost impossible to escape Auschwitz."

"He was selected to be what they called a *Sonderkommando,* the Jewish prisoners forced to move the people into the showers, pull their dead bodies out, burn them in the ovens, and then bury the ashes. It was the worst of all jobs, to have to betray your own people. They became complicit in the horror. They were there to keep order, to reassure the people that everything was okay. And they would be there until their usefulness was finished and then they would go the way of those they'd shepherded to their deaths.

"Your story about the red coat rings a bell with me. Abraham told me one of his first jobs at the camp was to sort through the clothes of the women and children who were sent to the showers, to look for hidden treasures, diamonds sewn in the hem of a coat, paper money or coins in the pockets, and so on. He came upon his wife's red coat in a pile and took a brief time to mourn her. Then he grabbed the coat, escaped on a burial detail, and joined the resistance. At that point he didn't care if he lived or died and wasn't afraid of getting caught. He told one of the other *Sonderkommandos* to say he had joined the line of victims into the shower because he didn't want to live without his wife and he couldn't do this job. That must have been how his name ended up on the list of murdered. That coat kept him warm on cold nights when he was on the run in the forest with the partisans. And the way he tells the story, there were diamonds and cash sewn into the hem of the coat which help fund partisan activities. He still carries a scrap of that red coat wherever he goes, as a reminder of his departed wife. He keeps it in a pocket of his coat or suit jacket or slacks. He even had it in his tuxedo when he married his second wife."

"I wonder how many times that happened in the war?" Hallelujah asked. "People lost to each other forever because of a cruel twist of fate."

"He spent many years alone until he finally remarried," Alexander explained. "His wife has since died, but he has spent decades trying to gain restitution from the German government for his losses and the losses of others. He works with the governmental organizations and the State of Israel to try to set things right. And he had the means to do it. But, like many victims, he hasn't been very successful. Many of his paintings have ended up in German museums, and there has been no proof that he ever owned them, until now. He started his business again after the war with money from the sale of the diamonds and the remainder of the cash sewn into the lining of that red coat. He was a smart man, and he built our firm into one of the world's top hedge funds. He will see that justice is done."

Alexander studied the list of items stolen from the Hammerman household, the paintings, antiques, and jewelry. Even the Hammerman mansion was appropriated by a Nazi officer.

Eva's eyes filled with tears. "Mr. Hammerman is alive? And he thinks his wife was killed during the war?"

"Yes, it was a great tragedy. He never stopped loving her."

"Nor she him," Eva added. "I know because I am still in touch with Madeline Hammerman. As a matter of fact, her granddaughter is a ballerina in New York, like she used to be. She will be coming to Berlin soon to perform in *Swan Lake*. Madeline is coming with the family, including her daughter, Ana, who is named after my mother. We have arranged a visit while she's on the continent."

Hallelujah reached out to touch Alexander's hand. "Do you realize what this means? That Mr. Hammerman's wife is still alive. And the girl must be his granddaughter. From a daughter he never knew he had. You could arrange for him to be at the performance."

"Of course I could arrange—"

Eva interrupted. "But what if it's a coincidence? What if it's the wrong Abraham Hammerman? It would be such a disappointment. To get one's hopes up and then have them come crashing down. It would be like losing her all over again."

"I don't believe in coincidences," Hallelujah said. "I believe God has had a hand in this, in helping us find you and these files"—she turned to Alexander—"and in helping us find each other."

He smiled. "I believe you're right. We must get back to Berlin right away to get this information into the right hands."

"But if someone is chasing us, why would you go back there?"

"That does not matter. We will do the right thing, no matter the cost. And Eva, will you testify to what you have written?"

"It's what I had always intended."

"Let me take notes on what I've heard today," Hallelujah said. "And will you tell us Madeline's story?"

"I would be happy to."

"I would like the world to know your stories. I would like to put them in a book. May I have your permission?"

Eva smiled. "I would love that."

Alexander shook Aaron's hand again and bent down to kiss Eva.

"Should I call you Eva or Hannah?"

"From now on, I think I am Hannah. It's been too long since she disappeared."

"Mother, what does he mean?" asked Aaron, who had been patiently listening to her tale. "Your name isn't Hannah."

"Son, it's a complicated story. One that is long

overdue to be told. Come closer. Let me tell you about your other family."

"Hannah," began Hallelujah, picking up one of the larger stones. "You should take one of the diamonds, perhaps for your Ana."

"My Ana is married, but her daughter is about to become engaged."

"Then please, take this. This should stay in the family."

Hallelujah placed the diamond in Hannah's hand, and her fingers closed around it. The old woman expelled a long breath.

"Hallelujah, let's let Hannah and her son have some time alone before you interview her. But before we go, I'd like to have a little word in private with her myself."

Hallelujah and Aaron left the room.

Chapter Seventeen
Madeline's Story: The War Years
*As told by Hannah Grandcoeur
to Hallelujah Weiss*

Life as she knew it, as a prima ballerina and a cherished young wife with an adoring husband, was over. Fate and her religion had landed her in this hell called Auschwitz, from which there was no escape.

Their plan to immigrate to America had gone up in smoke. Julian Hirschfeld had arranged it with Abe, but on the day they were due to leave, they were rounded up, told to bring only what they could carry, directed to the synagogue, and from there to an overcrowded train of terrified people headed to an undetermined location.

When Abe had asked why they were being deported, the SS man explained, "to work." That seemed to satisfy Abe. Work was a concept he understood. As long as they were able to work, they would be okay. In his mind, any obstacle could be overcome. She could tell he was putting up a front for her benefit, so she didn't tell him her news about the baby. Under normal circumstances, he would be thrilled, but a baby at this time would be a dangerous complication.

When they arrived at the camp, they were separated in the selection process. Abe went one way; she went another. It made sense to separate the men from the women and children. That was the Orthodox way. After all, they sat separately in the synagogue. But the moment her best friend's husband Julian was shot in the head, everything changed. In all of the chaos, she lost track of Abe. It was up to her to be strong and protect her unborn child. She'd tried to calm Ana, but her friend was distraught and half-mad, holding her screaming baby.

Madeline had to leave her new red coat outside the showers. She hated to do that. It had been a special gift from Abe, and there were diamonds and American dollars sewn in the hem, but there were men armed with machine guns and automatic rifles and fierce German shepherds patrolling the area. Barking dogs and men barking orders and armed men in the watchtowers left her no choice. They were told to leave their clothes in the undressing area, and that after their shower they would receive a meal and be given their work assignment.

Then, minutes before they were to enter the showers, a guard pulled her roughly out of line. "Come with me."

"Madeline," screamed Ana, who had never left her side. "Please, stay with us. Where are they taking you?" That was the last time she ever saw her friend.

Were they taking her to Abe? What did this mean? She could really use a shower after that long, grimy train ride. She was going to lose her place in line, and the guards were shouting to hurry, hurry, the water was getting cold. Maybe there was a mix-up in her papers. The guard knocked on the door of a barracks and turned her over to a female guard inside.

The woman perused her naked body

contemptuously. Then she directed her into the bathroom. "Clean up. There's bath soap, shampoo, powder, and perfume. You can use the makeup. There's a nightgown that should fit you, in the closet. Take whatever you need. You're a very lucky girl."

Madeline tilted her head in confusion. She didn't feel lucky. She and the others who had entered the work camp were being treated like dogs. Why was she being singled out? Right now, she craved the comfort of the crowd. Maybe it had all been a mistake. Well, if she was being freed, she would have to insist that Abe come along. For a moment, she thought she heard screams in the distance, but the scalding shower water drowned out the cries.

When she had toweled off, she walked into the closet and noticed that all the clothes were sheer nightgowns. She chose a deep rose silk gown. She picked up the brush on the dressing table, brushed out her hair, sniffed, and spritzed herself with the expensive perfume on the table. There was a pair of fluffy bedroom slippers in the closet, so she put those on. Now she was ready, but ready for what?

The female guard stepped into the room. "Come with me, now." Madeline followed her. They walked out the door to a waiting truck and drove outside the gate. Minutes later, the truck stopped, and she was taken into what looked like a small wooden house nestled in the woods and hurried into the bedroom.

"Wait here on the bed," the guard instructed.

Madeline did as she was told. What choice did she have? Five minutes later, a well-built blond-haired man, about her age, a man she might have found attractive under other circumstances, entered the bedchamber. He was in the uniform of the SS, very distinguished-looking. She rose when he came in. What was she supposed to do now? Did he expect her to bow? Salute? What was proper?

"Madam Hammerman," he began in a deep voice. "So nice of you to come."

Was the man crazy? He acted as if this were simply a social call and she had come of her own volition.

"You know who I am?"

"Of course. I've watched you perform many times. Most recently in *Swan Lake* at the Paris Opera Ballet." His eyes roamed her body, which was visible through the gown. Madeline blushed.

"You are even more beautiful in person. You have a dancer's body. It is very appealing to me."

Madeline bit her lip until it bled.

He walked up to her, and she could feel his breath on her neck. He caressed her body lightly with the pressure of his hands, outlining her breasts with her rosebud nipples, which he teased until they stood erect, curving around her stomach and then her buttocks.

She slapped him. "I am a married woman."

The man threw back his head and laughed and then caught her hand in his. "I could have you shot for that, or worse."

Madeline shrank back onto the bed.

"But I have you at a disadvantage," the man said politely. "I am SS-Hauptscharführer Maximillian von Gruber, part of the camp command. This is my house. You exist at my pleasure, and for my pleasure. I had hoped we could have a pleasant conversation over dinner, enjoy some delicious champagne, perhaps, and some rich chocolates? I have Swiss chocolates. How does that sound? And then we will discuss what I can offer you and what you can offer in return. I would like us to get better acquainted, if we might, *meine Dame*. May I call you Madeline? That is a lovely name. And you may call me Max. I have a proposition for you."

Madeline's eyes widened in confusion. "What kind of a proposition?"

"Auschwitz, the camp, can be a rather cold and unpleasant place, even a dangerous place. You will need someone to protect you."

"Against what?"

"Many things can happen here if one is not careful. Perhaps you've heard?"

Madeline shook her head. "This is my first night here."

"And I want it to be an enjoyable one. I can make that happen."

The man was polite, but his meaning was explicit. He was almost panting, like a dog. His erection was clearly outlined beneath his uniform.

"Do I have a choice?"

"My dear Madeline, of course you have a choice. I am not in the habit of forcing myself on women."

"I'm not interested in your proposition. Like I said, I am married."

"If we are being perfectly honest, I am married too, and I have two wonderful children back in Berlin. I haven't seen my wife in many months, and I have big appetites. And speaking of appetites—" He walked over to the door and called a guard. "You may bring in our dinner."

At his signal, a guard wheeled in a tray with a bottle of champagne cooling on ice, a carafe of water, a steaming roast pheasant, wild rice, roasted potatoes and, as promised, a bar of Swiss chocolate. The guard disappeared on command.

"Sit, please." He indicated a small table and chairs set for two. She sat and stared longingly at the food.

"I'm not hungry," she announced.

"You don't have to pretend with me. I know you have barely eaten since you were in Berlin, and you have had little water. Now, it would be a shame to waste such a lovely meal. So please eat with me."

Madeline was ravenous and thirsty. It was true. She hadn't had much to eat or drink in almost two days. She should keep up her strength for the baby's sake, until she could decide what to do. She nodded. Max smiled.

They ate in silence. Madeline was so hungry she practically wolfed down the food. The water landed like a balm on her chapped lips and parched throat, and the champagne made her tingle.

"Here, have another glass," said Max, who started to pour the champagne.

She hesitated.

"I insist. It's French. It will help you sleep."

Then he broke off a piece of chocolate and fed it to her.

It was heavenly.

"There, that's better. Now we can discuss our arrangement."

"I'd like to go back to my—my room, if you don't mind."

Max bellowed.

"Your room? Madeline, you will share your *room*, as you call it, and its thirty-six wooden bunkbeds, with five hundred other women. Let me enlighten you. There are no windows and no bathrooms. It's cold and unbearable, and you'll only have two meals a day—one cup of bitter coffee and a slice of bread in the morning, and some thin broth and bread in the evening. And beatings at the whim of your guards. If you try to escape, you'll be shot or hung. You are under the misconception that you have arrived at a first-class hotel. That is why I must protect you from harm. It is obvious you have delicate sensibilities. You can have this lovely home, where we can visit, have regular meals, enjoy a bit of music, exist in a state of seclusion. Perhaps you will even dance for me. And, when you get to know me better…"

"I would like to see my husband first," Madeline interrupted.

The SS man who called himself Max took a deep breath and spoke slowly.

"How does it feel to have your husband's life in your hands?"

Madeline shuddered.

"I think we understand each other. Now you should change your clothes, and I will have my guard escort you back to your quarters, where you can enjoy the hospitality of the camp for a few days. I wager you'll change your mind, then. I will send for you soon. Enjoy your grace period. Goodnight, Madeline."

Madeline discarded the flimsy nightgown and changed into the camp clothes provided for her. She breathed a momentary sigh of relief—until the guard returned and dragged her roughly out of the room.

Chapter Eighteen
Madeline

The next seven days were the worst week of Madeline's life. By the end of the "grace period," Madeline realized the truth about Auschwitz, the reality of the arbitrary beatings, shootings, and hangings, early morning roll calls in the dark, freezing weather, frequent and random selections, the starvation, disease, forced labor, and the ultimate terror—the "showers" and the ovens. Punishment was unexpected and harsh and as varied as the monsters who meted it out. If the victim died, what did that matter? There were always more unsuspecting people to torment, coming to the camp in an endless procession of humanity.

The stench of burning flesh could be smelled in the barracks, and the screams could be heard of the thousands of victims that streamed in daily, as they tried to escape being poisoned by exhaust fumes in the gas chambers. Rumors were that there were scratches on the concrete wall where people frantically clambered to get out. Ninety-nine percent of the Jews died within two hours of arrival. People didn't come there to work. Auschwitz was a killing factory.

It was incomprehensible, but true. Jews were rounded up in almost every city and town in Europe and transported to their deaths. Didn't anyone in the outside world know what was going on? Why didn't someone do something about it?

Madeline was physically sick. Being pregnant at Auschwitz was more than just an inconvenience; it was a death sentence. If you didn't die at the hands of the maniacal camp doctor, Josef Mengele, who had a penchant for torturing and experimenting on twins and pregnant women, your body would be worn out from lack of nutrition and being worked to death. You had to have a strong will to survive. And Madeline needed to survive, to protect her unborn child and reunite with her husband. She'd had no word of Abe since her arrival, but it was evident that her answer to the SS commander would seal her husband's fate, if he were still alive.

A week after she first encountered the SS officer, a guard came to get her out of the roll call line on a cold and rainy morning, when they'd been standing for hours, and brought her to the house in the forest.

What a difference a week made. She was filthy. Her scratchy work dress was wrinkled, dirty, and torn. It was no wonder. She worked and slept in the same outfit. There was no change of clothes. Her shoes barely fit, her hair was shaved off, and she bore a registration number tattooed on her left forearm. She was starving, thirsty, and freezing, and her toes nearly frostbitten. For a ballerina, that was the worst fate. But, luckily, her feet were already hardened from rigorous training and dedication to her art. She imagined what shape she would be in after a month, or a year, or for as long as this war dragged on. She could see the evidence when she stared into the gaunt faces of those who had managed to hang on. She now knew that being pulled out of the line to the showers had saved her life and the life of her unborn child.

She stood, utterly defeated, before the SS commander as he lounged nonchalantly in his chair. She would have gladly thrown herself on the electrified fence that surrounded the complex, including the killing center, but she had another life to consider.

"Madeline, so nice to see you again." His cruel smile lit up his face. "Have you reconsidered my offer? Are you ready to take advantage of my generous hospitality?"

At first, she was too furious to speak, but when she did, she kept her tone light. He was an insidious pig, but she would take what he had to offer, not for her sake but for her child's, and when she could, she would intervene to help others. If he wanted to play this cat-and-mouse game, then she vowed to beat him at it.

"I accept," she whispered.

"Speak up. I couldn't hear you."

"I said, I accept."

"I accept, *Max*," he chided.

"I accept, Max," she parroted in a monotone. The man was a beast masquerading as a human being.

Max got up from his chair and came around to where she was standing. He towered over her. He went to hug her but was obviously repelled by her appearance and, no doubt, her rancid smell.

"Why don't you wash up? You'll find clothes in the closet. I trust you'll have everything you need. It's a shame about your hair, but it will grow back." He looked her over. "Not too long, I hope." It was obvious he preferred her boyish appearance. He was conveying his unconventional proclivities loud and clear.

He didn't know she was pregnant, so she would have to sleep with him in order to convince him she was carrying his child. Surely he wouldn't kill the mother of his own child, and definitely not the child itself. It was a gamble, but then, her child's life depended on her ability to carry out this charade.

She took advantage of the opportunity to enjoy a hot shower, where she tried to scrub off all vestiges of the barracks. She shampooed and towel-dried her hair, what was left of it, and applied the makeup that was in the drawer. There was a closetful of clothes to choose from, all in her size. Abe had loved her long hair, but Max was right about one thing. It would grow back. She spritzed on some perfume in all the right places and realized how lucky she was. Not because she was being forced to act against her will, but because she surely wouldn't have survived another week in the barracks situation.

The door opened, and Max reentered the room. He came up behind her and wrapped her in a hug.

"You look lovely."

"I've looked better."

He turned her around and entreated her with his eyes.

"Madeline, I want to apologize for my behavior at our first meeting. That was not the way I wanted things to go. I didn't intend to be so heavy-handed. It's that I wanted to keep you safe. By sending you back to the barracks, I was taking a big chance. I couldn't always be there to protect you. Now I will find you a job doing cooking or light housekeeping, perhaps working in the storage warehouse in the sorting room, where you can grow out your hair and have more freedoms. I want you to enjoy our time together. I will do everything in my power to make you happy. I am not a fickle man. You will be the only one, while we're together. You have my word as an officer."

Madeline managed a smile. *The only one, besides your wife. And you're insane if you think I can enjoy myself while others are suffering around me. You can sugar coat this all you want, but you're a tyrant. You can shame me, but you will not bend me to your will. How much does your word mean?*

"Let's start with a healthy breakfast," he suggested. "You look like you're wasting away."

"I would like that," she admitted. He could probably hear her stomach growling. He called for a tray of hot food. "There are more clothes in your size in the closet. Feel free to use them. I've ordered books I think you'd like, and I have music. I have a busy day, but make yourself comfortable, and I will be back to visit you tonight. Perhaps you could dance for me. Meanwhile, I hope you can get some sleep while I'm gone. I want you to be rested for tonight. I'm looking forward to our arrangement, and I hope you are too. My assistant will bring you lunch, and we'll have dinner together. And don't worry. This will be our little secret. No one will have to know."

He turned to go, and then he reconsidered. "Oh, and Madeline, don't even think of escaping. I have posted guards outside, and they have orders to shoot on sight anyone who leaves this house unattended. But you'll be safe as long as you're in here under my protection." He smiled.

Then he walked out the door. Madeline knew that the camp was a hotbed of gossip. She just hoped Abe wouldn't hear about it. She devoured breakfast and then threw it up. It must be nerves or the pregnancy. She would have to hide that for the time being.

She walked into the closet. She knew where these clothes came from. They were from the sorting area—designated as *Canada*—where all the clothes worn by the victims passed through. Jewish prisoners, under the supervision of the SS guards and prison overseers, inspected each garment for diamonds, gold, jewels, coins, foreign currency, and other valuables. Anything of value would be stored in a box in the center of the barracks. The SS guards frequently helped themselves to the stolen goods. The SS guards were well fed and wanted for nothing, while the inmates in their charge were slowly wasting away. She had so much to eat and the other prisoners had nothing, but exhaustion overpowered her guilt and she fell asleep on the featherbed.

She must have slept through lunch, because she could see the full moon through the window. She got up, brushed her teeth, and picked out something to wear that was not too suggestive. Observing herself in the mirror, she looked almost demure.

The door opened. It was Max. Instead of his uniform, he had on casual clothes. He seemed happy to see her.

"You're wearing white. Perfect. Very symbolic. You are coming to me as a virginal bride."

No matter what she did, it seemed to excite him, albeit unintentionally.

"That's not exactly what I had in mind," she pointed out.

"Nevertheless. Our dinner should be arriving any minute."

"What would your wife think of this arrangement?"

"She will know nothing about it."

She wanted to bring up her husband, but she didn't think the time was right.

"Are you comfortable here?"

"It's an improvement over the prisoner barracks."

"Don't think of yourself as a prisoner."

"How should I think of myself, then?"

"As my very special guest."

"Do many of your compatriots have 'special guests'?"

"Although it's not officially sanctioned, yes, many do have their favorites."

He was charming in a sadistic kind of way. And she knew he was sadistic. She had experienced his mood swings firsthand. A few days ago, when a new transport arrived, she'd seen him shoot an old man who was limping and couldn't get in line fast enough. The man's body just lay there bleeding while everyone filed past. He was expendable, like every other prisoner. People had become inured to death. But she didn't point that out. She understood her purpose was to entertain Max and keep him on an even keel. She wanted to avoid another display of his temper. Like a viper, he could strike unexpectedly.

"Dinner was delicious," she said, wiping her mouth with the white napkin. "Thank you."

"You'll have to tell me what you like, and I'll make sure we have it on hand."

Such a polite conversation.

"So, I've brought some music—Tchaikovsky—and I thought you could dance for me. A private show."

"I'm a little out of practice." She thought Tchaikovsky an odd choice, since the Germans were locked in a death struggle with the Russians on the Eastern front.

"That won't be a problem. Practice makes perfect, does it not?" She didn't know if he was talking about dancing or other things.

She was just beginning to recover her strength. She wasn't sure she had the stamina to dance, but she didn't want to make waves, so she agreed.

He put on a record, and she danced. He was mesmerized. His eyes never left her body, and when the dance was done, he stopped the record and walked up to her.

"That was quite a performance."

"I am not wearing the right clothes for dancing."

He folded her in his arms and gently kissed her lips. "For what I have in mind, no clothes are required. Can we take the next step?"

He was asking her permission when they both knew he didn't have to.

She shuddered. "Whatever you'd like."

He went to the door and dismissed his guard. Then he locked the door and turned out the light.

"If you'd feel more comfortable, you may change in the bathroom. I'll be waiting in bed."

Madeline took a deep breath. This was the moment, then. She stepped into the closet and pulled out a diaphanous white nightgown and brought it into the bathroom.

When she came out, he was waiting for her in bed. He had removed his clothes, and when she approached the bed, he took her hand and pulled her against him.

"Madeline." He breathed her name and traced the outline of her body in the darkness before he began to undress her. He tenderly kissed her lips and then let his fingers explore, doing his best to prepare her. At one point he stuck one finger, then two, inside her, before he rolled her onto her stomach and entered her from behind.

She cried out. He ignored her cry and continued. Then he screamed in satisfaction at his release. After their interlude, he folded her in his arms.

"Have I hurt you?"

"It's just that I've never—"

"Ah. There are many things I can teach you, Madeline. I think you and I will get along just fine."

Fat tears slid down Madeline's face. Luckily, she was turned away from him, and he was already snoring.

When she woke up the next morning, Max was gone. She had breakfast alone.

Their meetings went on like this for months. He brought her several dance outfits—a romantic tutu like the ballerinas in the Degas painting in her home back in Berlin, tights and pink satin pointe shoes and a pair of soft leather ballet slippers.

One day he brought her a fluffy white dog he named Fritzy.

"She will keep you company when I'm gone." He treated that dog better than he treated the camp inmates. He pictured himself so cultured and refined, but he was the portrait of evil.

She danced for him often, and they "made love" in a variety of positions that Madeline had never been exposed to. By then her hair had grown out. Her stomach was beginning to show, so tonight she would break the news.

"Max," she began right before he drifted off to

sleep.

"Yes?"

"I have something to tell you, and I don't know how you are going to react."

She was worried. A pregnant mistress was an inconvenience. If he wanted to, he could have her sent to Dr. Mengele's laboratory, a special barracks where men and women were sterilized by horrible methods. The doctor particularly liked to experiment on pregnant women, she had heard. But she could no longer delay her announcement.

"What is it?"

"I'm pregnant. I haven't been using any protection, and I know you haven't."

Max sat up in bed.

"You're pregnant?" A look of disbelief swept across his face.

"That's what happens when two people—are together like we are."

She held her breath, expecting a violent reaction—steeled herself for a punch in the gut or a smack across the face. His gun was always out on the bedside table, a not-so-subtle threat to keep her in line and compliant.

"My God. Is it true? But this is wonderful news."

She released the breath.

"I thought you might be angry."

"Angry? No. You're right, this is what happens in the natural course of things. In the future we can take precautions, but I am overjoyed." He hugged her. "I will spend the entire night with you. You're carrying my child. I can't believe it. I love you, Madeline."

She wasn't expecting a declaration of love. She had half expected to be shot right then and there.

"Now we must make sure you eat right, have all the right things for the baby." He patted her stomach and fondled her breasts. "Yes, I notice the changes. I'll have the doctor come in and look at you."

"No," she cried. "Not the doctor."

Max smiled. "I know you have heard some things, and they are completely untrue. But I will have my personal doctor examine you. I wouldn't let that butcher Mengele touch you. You will not need to leave the room. Everything will be fine. The doctor I have in mind is very discreet. Let's just say this isn't the first time such a thing has happened."

They didn't talk about what would happen after the baby was born. Where would they live? How would she raise a child in confinement? Would he let her raise the child? While he was in such a good mood, she decided to risk asking him about Abe.

"Max. I have to know. I'm having your baby, and I'm married. Do you know anything about my husband, Abraham Hammerman?"

Max focused on a pattern in the carpet covering the floor. He finally looked up.

"I hate to have to break such sad news on this happy day, but your husband is dead."

Madeline's hands flew to her heart. She composed herself. "I have to ask. Did you have anything to do with this?"

Max looked offended. "I can't believe you would think that. Your husband was working on burial detail. He had a choice job. I saw to that myself. By all accounts, he was a good worker. He couldn't handle the assignment, and a witness said he walked right into the gas chamber. He committed suicide. It was a very noble act."

Madeline let out a silent scream and grabbed the bedpost. "How long have you known?"

"It happened soon after you got here. I should have told you."

Madeline clutched her belly and bit her lip to keep from screaming out loud. She didn't care if Max shot her. She couldn't stand the sight of him. "Would you please go now? I would like to mourn my husband in private."

"I understand. That is life. I'm sorry. I'll be by to check on you in the morning."

Max got dressed and walked out of the room. After he shut the door, Madeline collapsed on the bed and sobbed herself to sleep.

She hardened her heart against Max. Cold had seeped into her system and made a home there. If she ever got out of this place, she would never dance again.

But she and Max continued their hellish dance until the baby was born.

After the birth, she was allowed to nurse the infant, whom she named Ana, after her friend Ana Hirschfeld. They bonded, and the baby lived with them for a few months. Her figure had changed, and Max no longer desired her, but he was fascinated with his daughter.

He once asked, "Do you think she looks like her father?" and Madeline answered, "Most definitely." She was the picture of Abe, and that is what got Madeline through the ordeal. That time with her daughter was heaven.

When Max was transferred back to Berlin, he had the baby removed from the house and taken to a nearby farm to be raised by the farmer's wife. When Madeline begged him to take her and the baby to Berlin with him, he refused, although he did take Fritzy. He doted on that dog.

"I will miss you," he said.

She implored him to tell her where Ana was, and he said the baby was better off away from the camp and away from her, but he promised to come back and reunite them. When he finally did come back, she was already working at the brothel, and he installed a new female prisoner in his house. She was glad Abe wasn't alive to see what she had become. Would this war ever be over? Was her daughter still alive? Would she ever see her little Ana again?

****

Hallelujah put down her notes and flexed her aching hand. Tears streamed down her face.

"Madeline was a strong woman," Hallelujah commented. "I don't think I could have endured what she did."

"I've always thought so. But what choice did she have? What choice did any of our people have?"

"Hannah, what ever happened to Max?"

Hannah paused and looked out the window. "He was found guilty at the Auschwitz trial and sentenced to death by hanging. His sentence was carried out. He was executed in front of the crematorium in Auschwitz. It was a fitting end for him, I think."

Chapter Nineteen
Alexander and Hallelujah

AS THE PLANET SPINS SCRIPT EXTRACT
BY HALLELUJAH WEISS
SCENE 6. [IN PARKER'S OFFICE AT WINTHROP ENTERPRISES]
PARKER: So what's your answer? Are you going to marry me again?
POLLY: Do I have your word that you'll be faithful? And that you're going to sack your secretary?
PARKER: I'll have to find her another job.
POLLY: Fine with me, as long as it's with another company, preferably in another city.
PARKER: Done and done.
POLLY: (ADMIRING HER NEW ENGAGEMENT RING) Parker, you're not the most trustworthy man in the world, but you stood by me when I was in a coma for a year, and you never gave up hope. Although you did take up with that model while I was unconscious.
PARKER: I thought you'd forgiven me for that. I was so distraught. And so lonely. And as long as we're speaking of trust, what about the time you lied when you told me Patricia was Lance's daughter?
POLLY: Lance falsified the paternity test results. He never told me.
PARKER: I missed a lifetime with our Patricia.
POLLY: I thought we'd moved past that. We both have

our trust issues, but I do love you, so, yes, I'm willing to take a risk and give you another chance.
PARKER: [EMBRACING POLLY] I love you too, Polly.

****

Alexander and Hallelujah strolled along a path in a lush park in Baden's Old Town. In a way, Baden reminded him of Berlin, the old and the new, side by side, the diverse shops and restaurants, the spa district, and the breathtaking views, giving the city an international air. Caught up in the moment, Alexander reached for Hallelujah's hand. A brief look of suspicion clouded her face. Then she relented and clasped his hand as they continued their walk.

"Hallelujah, I'd like to talk to you about something."

"That sounds serious."

"It is. It's about us. And our future together. I was going to wait, to convince you to come to Berlin, but this can't wait. Sometimes we have to seize the opportunity."

Hallelujah had a sense she knew where this conversation was going, and she had to stop him before he traveled down that path and said things he couldn't take back.

"You know we have nothing in common," Hallelujah remarked. "You love math. I detest it. You want to live in Germany. I wouldn't go there for any amount of money. Your parents want you to marry a proper German girl and have proper German children. You want to bring home a Jew. I'm a risk-taker like Polly. And you're…methodical. Have you ever done anything spontaneous in your life?"

Alexander smiled. He was about to do something very spontaneous. Not exactly spontaneous. He had been thinking about it since their wedding…well, their pseudo wedding. And he had been making plans. He was a big planner. And Hallelujah was right. He was methodical. But you had to be methodical if you wanted to get what you were after. And he was after Hallelujah.

He pulled Hallelujah down to sit on a bench. He palmed her face and turned it toward him.

"I tossed a bag of diamonds to a stranger on a plane. That's pretty spontaneous, wouldn't you agree?"

"I've been wondering why you did that. Why did you pick me, of all the people on the plane?"

"I saw your face and looked into your eyes, and it just felt right. It was like a lightning strike."

"That's the way it was for Parker and Polly," Hallelujah admitted. But somewhere in the back of her mind she acknowledged that Parker and Polly weren't real. She was living in a Hollywood fairy tale, and she needed to clear the cobwebs.

Hallelujah shook her head dismissively and shook off Alexander's hand.

"You have a house that you're rehabbing for a family. You even have a nursery, and you don't even have a wife or a child. Who does that? You're either very optimistic or you're incredibly delusional."

As soon as the words were out, Hallelujah regretted them. He had remodeled his home for Sigrid and her baby, a baby he'd thought was his.

Alexander lowered himself to one knee in front of Hallelujah.

"I'm not delusional," he said evenly. "A delusional person believes things that couldn't possibly be true.

You are the truest thing I've ever known. I believe in us. I knew you were the one the minute I saw you. I love you, Hallelujah Weiss Evans, back to Weiss."

Alexander held out a diamond. An exquisite diamond that shone in the sunlight. It was a large, emerald-cut diamond. The kind of diamond Parker would give to Polly. The kind of diamond she and Polly adored.

"Alexander, this is one of the Hirschfeld diamonds."

"Yes, it is. I offered to buy it from Hannah for any amount of money, but she refused. She wanted me to have it. She wanted us to have it. She asked me if you were my sweetheart. And I told her I planned to marry you. She insisted, and she wouldn't take money from me. Of course, I'll get it properly set and then give it back to you. Hallelujah, will you marry me?"

Hallelujah looked into Alexander's gray eyes.

There. He'd gone and done it. Surprised her, and with Hannah's diamond. The words were out. Could she dash his hopes? Could she crush hers?

"Resistance is futile," Alexander said, thinking he had her. He knew, at any rate, he wasn't going to take No for an answer. He was so close. But she hadn't given him an answer.

"I'm not very good marriage material," Hallelujah protested. "I've been married more times than you can imagine."

Alexander laughed. "I think you're confusing yourself with Polly."

Hallelujah blinked. "Well, *I'm* not a very good risk either."

"Evaluating risk is my business. I'll take my

chances."

"I can hardly bring you home to my parents," Hallelujah pointed out. "You're German, and my father's a rabbi, for heaven's sake, a Holocaust-obsessed rabbi. He's written books on the subject. Every one of his sermons references the Holocaust. To him, the Holocaust is the root of all evil."

Alexander had been prepared for this.

"I've already asked your father for permission."

Hallelujah's eyes widened in surprise. "And what did he say?"

"He thought it was rather sudden, after your divorce, and he wanted to know if I loved you. He didn't ask about my nationality."

"And do you really love me?"

"The word 'love' doesn't do justice to what I feel for you. I feel as if my whole life has opened up and my heart is swelling and I can barely breathe when I'm around you. Like I've been underwater in the dark and I've finally surfaced into the light. I love you so much it hurts. Since I met you, I can't imagine life without you. I never thought love would be this wonderful. I had hoped. When I told your father how I felt, he said it sounds like it's *bashert*. Is that a good thing?"

"Yes, that's Yiddish for 'meant to be.' It's like fate, like the universe is saying we belong together, that it is pulling us together."

"He said sometimes something good comes out of a bad experience, like your divorce."

"I find it hard to believe that Rabbi Jacob Weiss would welcome a German to the family with open arms. His parents perished in the Holocaust. My mother's family lost people in the Holocaust, too. They take the credo 'Never Again' very seriously."

"You know that all Germans aren't Nazis. Just because my parents are German, which makes me part German, I hope you won't paint me with the same broad brush."

"That's fair, but you still have to go through the *rebbetzin*."

"The *rebbetzin*?"

"Yes. The rabbi's wife, otherwise known as my mother. She's going to be a tough sell. She still hasn't forgiven God *or the Germans* for the Holocaust. Has she given her permission?"

"Well, no."

"Then there's the issue of children," Hallelujah responded. "I know you want children. If I had children, I'd have to raise them in my faith."

Hallelujah inhaled a deep breath. That was the crux of the issue, wasn't it? It all came down to the children, and passing on the legacy of 4,000 years of Jewish existence, heritage, and values. How many times had her father said, "Don't break the chain of Jewish continuity, the bond of Jewish culture. The tree of Judaism must continue to grow and flourish. We must preserve our faith."

As a rabbi's daughter, she was raised to believe that, and she did believe it. Memories of her childhood came streaming back. Sitting on her father's lap on the *bimah* during Shabbat services. Listening to her mother singing in the synagogue choir. The aroma of chicken soup boiling on the stove and brisket in the oven, the sweet taste of challah and apples and honey. Celebrating all the holidays throughout the year. Memories and traditions she wanted to pass on to her children; memories, in turn, that they would share with their children. It had never occurred to her to marry someone who wasn't Jewish. But now, a man she'd practically just met was asking her to betray her faith. Of course, she had married Lloyd, and look what happened there. Just because someone was Jewish didn't make him a nice person.

What was Alexander's religion? She'd never even asked, but regardless, she knew how she wanted her children to be raised, and she wouldn't compromise. Especially after learning Hannah Hirschfeld's story. Hannah, a woman who was forced to deny her religion her whole life. Hallelujah was not going to do that to any children she might be blessed with, and she told Alexander so.

"And I would never ask you to do that. Our children will be raised as you wish." So, they were of the same mind on that subject. "Of course, I hope they don't turn out to be banshees like Ivan the Terrible or Vlad the Impaler."

"That could be a problem," she agreed.

"Well?" he coaxed, his eyes pleading with her.

What would Polly do? If truth be told, right now she didn't give a damn what Polly would do. She had a mind of her own, didn't she? Anyway, Polly was in love with Parker. And she was in love with Alexander. Her instinct was to grab onto this bit of happiness and never let go.

"How do I answer you? I already said, 'I do.' "

Alexander broke out into a sunny smile. "A definite Yes would be nice."

"First, I have to ask. What does your secretary look like?"

Alexander smiled. He was aware of Hallelujah's fears about the other woman.

"*He* wears horn-rimmed glasses and suspenders, has a five-o-clock-shadow, and his name is Rudolf. Not my type, so no worries there. And, as I said before, I'm not your ex-husband."

"Am I that obvious?"

"No one's ever been jealous over me before. I kind of like it. Any other objections I can overcome?"

"We have to be married in a synagogue," she insisted. "You probably don't have any left in Berlin."

"Another misconception. There are more than a hundred and ten synagogues in Germany. As a matter of fact, we have more synagogues than Jews."

Hallelujah cocked her head suspiciously.

"That's a joke. You see, Germans do have a sense of humor. That they don't is another misconception. Actually, Germany is home to the eighth largest Jewish community in the world."

"How many Jews are there in Berlin?" Hallelujah asked pointedly.

"Maybe thirty thousand in Berlin and about a quarter of a million in Germany. We have some beautiful synagogues in Berlin," Alexander said. "There's the *Neue* or New Synagogue, on *Oranienburger Strasse* in Central Berlin. It was constructed in 1866 and left in ruins after Kristallnacht and the allied bombing of Berlin. It's been restored and now is a liberal place of worship and a memorial and museum with a permanent exhibition tracing the history of the synagogue. We could get married on the top floor there. I think the rabbi would marry an interfaith couple.

"There are a lot of monuments you might be interested in seeing when we get to Berlin. There's the Jewish museum and an outdoor Holocaust Memorial, near the Brandenburg Gate and the new American Embassy, called the Memorial to the Murdered Jews of Europe, which consists of two thousand seven hundred eleven slabs of gray concrete, some rising as high as thirteen feet. I think you'll be surprised. We'll fly your parents over."

"I never agreed to live in Berlin."

"Will you at least give it a chance? I think it would be a wonderful tribute if we raised our family in the Hirschfelds' home. A new generation, out of the ashes."

"I understand there is a rise in anti-Semitic incidents and sentiment in Berlin, and neo-Nazi groups throughout Germany."

"We have many problems to confront, many issues to solve, and not all our people have learned from the past," admitted Alexander. "But there is a rebirth of sorts in Berlin. We have a very active Jewish community. We could start by building a bridge."

Hallelujah sighed. She supposed she could go to Berlin, see the house, test her comfort level in the city. If she felt the least bit threatened, then that would be a deal-breaker. Tipping the scales was the way she felt about Alexander, the way her heart expanded every time she looked at him. The way she couldn't look away. The feeling that they belonged together, that this *was* a match made in heaven. As though he were a *stolperstein*, she had stumbled upon Alexander, the one man she was meant for. And together, they would find the right path.

She jumped into Alexander's arms.

"Is that a Yes?" he asked hopefully.

Hallelujah laughed. "It's a definite Yes."

Alexander kissed his bride and hugged her.

"Well, we've already had our honeymoon. So I guess we need to fulfill our promise to Hannah. It won't be easy. It might be dangerous."

"Nothing worth doing is ever easy, and we'll be doing it together."

Chapter Twenty
Hallelujah

When they arrived at the airport in Berlin, Hallelujah crossed her arms, narrowed her eyes, and listened to the cacophony around her. Everything sounded guttural in German. It was a strange language.

"Nervous?" Alexander asked.

"A little. I feel like I'm going to be arrested by the Gestapo any minute."

"That's ridiculous. You're just not used to the German language."

"I feel like I'm out of place, like I'm not wanted here."

"You are wanted, by me."

Hallelujah watched the guards patrol the perimeter of *der Flughafen*. Even the word "airport" sounded ominous in German.

"Where are we going now?"

"Home, to my place."

"But the people who tried to kill you know where you live. It's not safe. And we have the diamonds and all of Hannah's documents. The banks aren't open this time of night."

"It's safe enough. I have to warn you, though, I don't know how much progress the contractors made since I left. It should be almost finished, but I can't guarantee what the place looks like."

"Why can't we stay at a hotel? Then no one would know where we are. And we'd have time to figure out our next step."

"That makes a lot of sense. If it would make you feel more comfortable, we can do that. I know just the place. The Hotel Adlon Kempinski. It's a five-star luxury hotel on *Unter den Linden*—that means 'under the linden.' The linden are lime trees. It's right in the heart of the city, where all the spies stayed during World War II, at least according to the novels I've read."

"That's comforting. Too bad I didn't bring my trench coat."

"You don't need a trench coat to enjoy Berlin. And when I show you around, I think you'll fall in love."

She already had. But not with the city.

Alexander handed her out of the cab and checked them into the hotel. He asked the bellman to bring their luggage to the room, but he held on to the diamonds.

"Let's have tea in the lobby lounge and bar. It's a real treat. The owner has a passion for food. We could have coffee or tea, or champagne, or something sweet from the *pâtisserie*. The cakes and tarts are delicious. And we have to try the apple strudel with vanilla sauce."

He led her to a seating arrangement by the iconic elephant fountain. "This hotel has quite a legendary history."

When they were seated, Alexander read from the menu, translating to learn her preferences. He ordered in German.

Somehow when Alexander spoke the language it didn't sound so threatening.

"Are you staying at the hotel?" the server asked.

"Yes, my wife and I just checked in. We're in room 305. You can charge our room."

"May I see your papers?"

Hallelujah's brows shot up.

Alexander handed them his hotel receipt.

"Welcome to the Hotel Adlon Kempinski." The server left to get their waters.

"Did that woman just ask us to show our papers to have a pastry?"

"It's not what you think," Alexander assured. "She just wanted confirmation of our room number so she can put the charge on our room. We'll get settled after our snack, rest a bit, and then there's an amazing Italian restaurant I want to take you to."

"Italian food? In Germany?"

"Oh, yes. There are several wonderful Italian restaurants that are so authentic you'd think you are in Italy. *Il Punto* and *Bocca Di Bacco*. You will be very surprised. I've been wanting to take someone there, a date, for instance, but I haven't had a chance, not since Sigrid. I take out most of my meals from the *KaDeWe*, the *Kaufhaus Des Westens*, near the *Kurfürstendamm* boulevard. There's a gourmet food hall on the sixth floor. It is the biggest and best department store in Germany, sort of like Harrods. It has cheeses, chocolate, about four hundred kinds of bread, and every kind of food you could ever imagine."

"You eat dinner at a department store?"

"It gets lonely sometimes, eating alone."

Hallelujah put a hand on Alexander's.

"But now that I have you…"

Hallelujah smiled.

Alexander's voice raised in excitement. "We can take the hop-on, hop-off bus around the city. There are so many things I want to show you. And strolling down the *Unter den Linden* at night is so romantic. We'll pass by many landmarks. You can still see remnants of the Wall. As a matter of fact, you can see evidence of the Wall everywhere, either pieces of the Wall or double rows of bricks on the street or pavement, which indicate where the Wall was at one time."

"How about Gestapo Headquarters?"

Alexander frowned. "Yes, that is also a tourist attraction now. It's called *Topographie des Terrors*, and it's at the site of the former Gestapo and SS Headquarters. It details crimes at the excavated torture cells. And there's an original section of the Berlin Wall on view that used to run just behind the building. I'd prefer we not see that until you've had a chance to appreciate the beauty of Berlin, though."

A siren sounded outside the hotel. Berlin hadn't changed the song of its sirens since the Second World War. Hallelujah folded her arms. She was afraid she was going to be rounded up.

She knew Alexander could read her thoughts. "You're not going to make this easy, are you? In your mind, we're all guilty until proven innocent. Won't you at least give the city a chance?"

Hallelujah didn't answer. Then she narrowed her eyes and lowered her voice, affecting a German accent. "We have ways of making you talk."

"That's not fair."

"Tell me, do you plan to spend the rest of your life in Berlin? I think I have the right to know."

"No, eventually I want to go back home. And the

time to go may be sooner than you think. We're a big player in the hedge fund space, but it's been a rough year. There's a lot of uncertainty. Some clients are pulling back because of fees. Pension funds are pulling out, and there's been a reassessment. Money is moving into ETFs. Our revenues missed their estimates. We're not exactly outperforming internationally, but I really love what I do."

"And I love what I do."

"But you can write soap operas from anywhere in the world. And you need to write your novel now that you have your high-concept idea."

"True, but I came for a short vacation. I never imagined it would turn into a lifetime."

Alexander turned to face her.

"But that's what I'm asking for, Hallelujah, a lifetime."

He pulled her close.

"Okay. I promise to give you and your city a chance."

"There's a great panoramic view from the Berlin TV Tower. And we're right around the corner from the Neo-Classical Brandenburg Gate, one of the few remaining historic city gates. It's the city's most famous landmark. Did you know more than seventy percent of Berlin was destroyed during the war?"

"I didn't know that."

"And, oh, I want to take you to the *Tiergarten*. We call it the Green Lung of Berlin. It was once a royal hunting estate, and it's now a park. Berlin is one of Europe's greenest capital cities. The *Tiergarten* was totally reforested after people cut down every tree to burn for firewood at the end of the war."

Alexander was a walking, talking advertisement for the city. It was hard not to get caught up in his contagious enthusiasm.

"It all sounds very exciting, except for the fact that when we get back to your house, we'll be sitting targets."

"I'd almost forgotten," said Alexander, checking his coat pocket for the package of diamonds.

"Too bad you're not carrying a gun in that pocket. I can't wait until the bank opens tomorrow and you can unload those stones. I'll sleep a little easier."

Talking of sleeping, Hallelujah noticed that Alexander had reserved only one room. He'd been so used to the two of them sleeping together onboard the ship that it must have slipped his mind. They hadn't actually consummated their marriage, their fake marriage. But anything could happen tonight.

Chapter Twenty-One
Julian Hoffman

"You're where?"

"I've been detained at the airport in Stockholm. But it's all a big misunderstanding. I'll be back in Berlin soon. It was the girl's fault. She told the police I was carrying a bomb. And once they found out I wasn't, those two had already gotten away."

Julian gripped his cell phone and tried to gain control of his temper. He wasn't known for his patience.

"So you lost them again?"

"The last I saw, they were approaching the security line. I have no idea where they were flying to."

"Then it's a good thing you're not in charge of this operation. If there's one thing I can't abide, it's incompetence. I checked the flights, and they have already landed in Berlin, but they could be anywhere. Berlin is a big city."

"I'll check Stone's house when I get back."

"I already have someone watching the house. Don't you think I'd know if they were there?"

"Did you check the hotels?"

"That's my next step. They can't get away. Get on a plane and come to my office as soon as you land. We need to find these amateur renegades."

Chapter Twenty-Two
Alexander

Alexander paused on the pavement outside the entrance to his house while he watched the cab pull away.

"Come," he said to Hallelujah. "Look down, and you can see the stumble stones."

Hallelujah knelt down on the pavement and waved her hand reverently over each of the plaques, touching them one by one—Julian, Ana, Hannah, and Aaron Hirschfeld.

"They're beautiful," she whispered.

"Yes. This is where it all started and ended."

"It's like they're still with us. This is their resting place. They're back home."

They carried their luggage down the walkway. Alexander put down his rollerbag, unlocked the door, and swept Hallelujah into his arms.

"What are you doing?"

"Carrying my bride across the threshold."

"I'm not really your bride."

"Not yet, but this is the first time you've seen my house, and I want to do things properly."

Hallelujah put her arms around Alexander's neck, and he deposited her gently in the foyer and looked at her expectantly.

"Well, what do you think?"

Hallelujah walked into the huge space.

"Alexander, it's amazing. I guess they've finished construction. Wow, I didn't expect it to be so grand. It's lovely. The skylight and the windows... There's so much light."

Alexander smiled. "I'm glad you like it. I tried to maintain the original style. I had a decorator in to update the bathrooms and reconfigure some spaces."

"It's just like Hannah described. I wish we could bring her here. This was the home she was born in and lived in, until—"

"Yes, until. But let's don't dwell on the past. We have our whole future ahead of us. Let me show you around on the first floor and upstairs."

"Is it safe? I mean, don't the people following you know where you live?"

"Yes, but I'm not going to let anyone chase us from our home."

Our home. Hallelujah rolled the words around in her mind. "You sound very sure of yourself."

"I've had a top-of-the-line security system installed. And I've reported the break-in to the police, so they'll be on the alert. I don't think the same people will try to break in again."

"I disagree. For a fortune in diamonds, I think they would do anything."

Alexander held her hand, and they walked around the first floor, with Hallelujah making a fuss over each room.

"You have a ballroom! Imagine that! What a fabulous place to entertain."

"I don't really have an occasion to use it, but it was so beautiful I didn't want to change it."

"And the kitchen is so spacious and modern. I'm not the world's greatest cook, but I could learn to cook in a kitchen like this. Why didn't you tell me you live in a mansion? And this library—it's wonderful."

He led her up the winding marble staircase. She had a good feeling about this place. She might be able to live here.

The master suite was magnificent.

"This house is like something out of a fairy tale. It feels like it was built for a princess."

"It was. Hannah was her father's little princess."

He led her down a long hallway. "And this is the nursery."

Hallelujah blushed. "I think you might be getting ahead of yourself."

"I don't think so. I like to be prepared. You have to have a plan. There's plenty of room for visitors, and there's an office on the other side of the master suite with a view of the Spree River. It was going to be my office, but you can write there. I'll be fine in the library. And I'm saving the best for last—the conservatory on the top floor. It has the most lovely view."

"You've thought of everything."

"I need to go to the bank, and there's another errand I have to run. So take your time unpacking and getting settled. The housekeeper stocked the kitchen and changed the sheets in our bedroom."

Hallelujah sighed. "Our bedroom?"

"Yes, I hope you will get used to the idea and love the place as much as I do. You will love the closet. It's cavernous, with plenty of room for your things. I know women love big closets." She could appreciate Alexander's positive take on that.

"I won't be long. You can set up your computer in the office if you'd like to work on your scripts or start your novel. There's a spare key on the table in the hallway downstairs. But don't go out without me. When I get back, we'll go to dinner."

"Thank you." Hallelujah carried her laptop into the spacious office. On the way, she passed the bedroom. Last night she and Alexander had been too exhausted to do anything but fall asleep on the hotel bed. But she knew that one night, soon, she and Alexander were finally going to make love. And she could hardly wait.

She heard his footsteps on the stairs and the door as it closed, so she got to work on the next episode of *As the Planet Spins* and started an outline for her novel.

Chapter Twenty-Three
Alexander

Alexander retrieved the large diamond from a pouch in his pocket and placed it on the glass countertop. His plan to return to the jewelry store that had conducted the appraisal was risky, but it was the only way to force the *Gruppen* out of hiding.

"This is magnificent," the jeweler exclaimed. "As I recall, this is one of the diamonds I appraised for you earlier, the Hirschfeld cut." He examined it under his jeweler's loupe.

"Yes, it is. And I need to find the perfect platinum setting for an engagement ring."

"Your fiancée is a very lucky woman." He measured the stone. "This stone is six carats. And it's flawless."

"I think I'm the lucky one."

"Look around and see if you see something you like. We have some lovely settings that will fit this stone. Or we can have one designed."

"No, I'd rather not wait." Alexander walked around the counter and picked out a platinum antique setting. "Would this work?"

"You have exquisite taste, Mr. Stone."

"Thank you." The jeweler picked up the setting and let Alexander examine it.

"This is the one. How soon can you have it ready?"

"Well we're about to close, so how about tomorrow morning? Can you leave it with me?"

"That will work. And yes, but I don't have to tell you how valuable the piece is."

"I understand," said the jeweler.

Alexander walked out of the jewelry store humming.

****

As soon as his customer left, the jeweler picked up the telephone.

"Julian, this is Otto. Your man was just in the store, and he had one of the Hirschfeld diamonds with him. He's getting it set as an engagement ring. I thought you'd want to know."

"Did he bring the rest of the diamonds?"

"I didn't see them. I told him to come back tomorrow morning to pick up his order."

"Excellent. I will be waiting. Mr. Stone must be back at his house, which is right around the corner from your shop."

"Glad I could be of help."

"And when I do collect the rest of the order, I can use your help disposing of them."

"The happy couple or the diamonds?" the jeweler wanted to know.

Julian laughed. "Both."

Chapter Twenty-Four
Hallelujah

"Hallelujah?"

"I'm upstairs," she called, rising from her desk and stretching. "You were gone a long time."

"I stopped by the office to make some calls. I made us a reservation at a neighborhood trattoria."

"Italian again? I'm not complaining, mind you. I could eat pasta every night."

"I know. Anything happen while I was away?"

"No, it was perfectly quiet. I got a lot done. I could work here."

"I'm glad."

He kissed her on the lips, took her hand, and they walked down the stairs.

"The restaurant is not far from here."

They walked out the door, and Alexander set the alarm.

It was a crisp night. The stars were bright in the sky. The moon was full. It was lovely.

"The food at the restaurant is very good, and it's right in the neighborhood. You know, after Sigrid broke up with me, I used to walk by this restaurant and look at all the happy couples inside and wish I had someone to eat there with. And now I have you." He squeezed her hand.

"I think Sigrid made a big mistake. You're pretty

hot. I'm probably going to have to keep a close eye on you."

"Most girls just find me boring. All I talk about is work, and that's a turnoff."

"You're not that way with me. I like the fact that you have a big brain. I find you fascinating."

"I guess when you're in love, that's the way it is."

"I guess so."

They walked into the restaurant.

"Reservation for Stone."

They were led to an intimate table in a glassed-in garden.

"This is very romantic," said Hallelujah.

The server handed them the menus and recited the specials.

"I'll have spaghetti with white clam sauce," said Hallelujah after studying the menu.

"Make mine the lasagna. Hallelujah, would you like red or white wine?"

"I'll have a glass of Moscato d'Asti."

"Bring us a bottle of your Moscato," Alexander said. The server left to fill their drink order.

"So what did you have to take care of at work?"

"I don't want to bore you, just playing catch-up."

"What about your errands?"

"Well, that's a surprise."

"Hmm. You are full of surprises."

The server brought the wine, and they made a toast.

"Just think. A few days ago we were on a ship," said Hallelujah. "Sometimes it feels like we're still swaying."

"I think that's the Moscato talking."

The food arrived, and it was delicious.

"I think the food here is as good as it is in Italy," she remarked.

"I'm not a connoisseur of Italian food, but it tastes good to me."

After dinner, they strolled around the neighborhood. When they got back to the house, they looked at the stumble stones, glowing in the moonlight.

"What a lovely tribute," Hallelujah said. "I love the idea of the stumble stones."

"Me too."

As they walked up to the house, Hallelujah exclaimed, "Oh, no, Alexander, look." Her body shook as she pointed to the wall.

He looked up and saw a hastily painted swastika dripping in blood red against the white stucco, illuminated by the moon and the front porch light. Beside the swastika were two messages: "Kill the Jews" and "Jews to the Gas." He drew her to him.

"Don't look," he said, gritting his teeth and whipping out his cell phone. "I'll have my construction team out to remove it. It will be gone in the morning. I'm calling the police."

"It's a warning, to me."

"I hate that you had to see that."

"I hate that they ruined your beautiful new home."

"*Our* home. This was not the welcome to my city I had in mind."

"Does this happen often?"

"I've never seen it before."

"I have. Back home. It's not uncommon. Someone once burned a swastika on our lawn. My father's answer was to gather the congregation and the town leaders together, a coming-together moment, he called it. I think it's the work of cowards. I suspect that deep down no one has changed. I told him he was wasting his time, and his answer was that forgiveness and understanding are never a waste of time."

"Let's go inside."

"Do you think they got into the house?"

Alexander punched in the alarm code and looked around. "It doesn't appear that they did."

He locked the door and led her into the kitchen, offering her a glass of hot cocoa.

"I hope you won't let this influence your decision to stay."

"On the contrary. They don't know me. I'm stubborn. It just helped me make up my mind. If I want to stay in Berlin, I will stay. No one is going to chase me away. We have an obligation to the Hirschfelds and to the other survivors. This is our home and their home, too, and I refuse to leave."

Chapter Twenty-Five
Alexander and Hallelujah

Alexander walked into the jewelry store and was greeted by the owner. "Do you have the ring ready?"

"Yes. Why don't you come in the back with me, and we can look at it together."

"The back?" In Alexander's admittedly limited experience of buying jewelry, he had never heard of conducting business in the back of the shop. That should have been a red flag. He was beginning to get a bad feeling.

Noting his customer's consternation, the jeweler responded, "Only our best customers get to see the back room. Come."

Still wary, Alexander followed the jeweler into the back through a steel door, and into a storeroom of sorts.

"I will be right back with your ring," the jeweler announced. "Have a seat." He indicated a side chair. Not a very comfortable side chair. In front of the chair was a small table and opposite him on the other side of the table was another chair. There was a naked bulb hanging from the ceiling. It looked more like an interrogation room than a jewelry store.

Alexander waited for about ten minutes and had just started to get up when a man walked into the room. He was short and stocky, and very well dressed.

"Mr. Stone, I am glad to make your acquaintance. I

am Julian Hoffman." He shook Alexander's hand and pulled out the chair opposite Alexander's.

"Where is Herr Weber?"

"He's currently with a customer. I'm here to talk to you about the diamond you brought in. The Hirschfeld diamond."

Alexander's mouth opened in surprise. "How do you know about that?"

"Herr Stone—or should I call you Alexander? You'll find that there's not much I don't know about many things."

Alexander started to rise again but was stopped by a firm hand on his shoulder.

"We have some unfinished business, Herr Stone," the man said smoothly. "That diamond was part of a group of diamonds promised to my father during the war and never delivered."

"I don't understand," Alexander said.

"I think you do. You are currently living in the house that my father, Franz Hoffman, used to own. The diamonds were hidden in that house when he sold it. My father is dead. Therefore, those diamonds belong to me."

So this was Herr Hoffman's son with Eva. He looked like a mob boss.

"I don't know what you are talking about."

"Let me see if I can refresh your memory."

Alexander eyed the door in case he had to make a quick getaway. He was younger and taller than Herr Hoffman, but the villain was stronger.

Julian smiled.

"If you're thinking of screaming or escaping, let me assure you that the door is made of steel, and no one can hear us. So, where were we? Ah, yes, we were discussing the diamonds. Let us put our cards on the table, so to speak." At that point, he removed a gun from his jacket pocket and placed it on the table between them.

Alexander's eyes bulged. "Are you threatening me?"

"That is the furthest thing from my mind. I am not a killer, Mr. Stone. Far from it. I run a very lucrative import/export business. No need for alarm. You're a businessman. I'm a businessman. I think we can conclude our transaction very easily."

"I have only the one diamond. It's for my fiancée's engagement ring."

"If that's the case, then you'll be free to leave with your diamond. But I am afraid that is not the case," said Julian, fingering the gun. "I know you found a bag of diamonds, diamonds with very specific marks, because you brought them in to Herr Weber to have them appraised. Then they were stored in your bank safe deposit box. After which you took them on a plane to Rome, where you met the very beautiful Hallelujah Weiss, boarded a cruise ship, and now you are back in Berlin."

"Keep Hallelujah out of it."

Julian rubbed the metal of the handgun.

"I'm afraid your fiancée is very much in it, up to her very Jewish neck."

"Was it you who painted the swastika on my house?"

"Not me personally. I generally do not get my hands dirty. But I might make an exception for the lovely Hallelujah."

Alexander jumped up. "My fiancée doesn't scare easily."

"We will soon see if that is true. And I wouldn't run, if I were you. My men are right outside that door. Besides, I would blow a hole in your head before you reached the door. I am a very good shot. And then where would Hallelujah be? Right now, I know exactly where she is because I have some men outside your house with instructions to bring her to me. So you will be reunited with your lovely bride-to-be before you know it."

Alexander sat down on the chair.

"I hope you are not going to make the same mistake as Herr Hirschfeld did. He refused to give my father the diamonds he promised, and regrettably he and his family and many of their friends paid the ultimate price. He did not take my father seriously."

"Certainly we are no longer in Nazi Germany. And his entire family did not pay the price. I believe your mother survived the ordeal."

Julian flinched. "What do you know about my mother?"

"I met with your mother in Baden, Switzerland. You didn't know that, did you? You underestimate your mother. She is a very brave woman. She sacrificed a lot to get the proof to put your father and his illicit organization away. She gave me some documents that can expose your entire operation."

"My mother knows nothing about my operation."

"That's where you're wrong. When she was married to your father, she kept detailed records of all the transactions, including paintings, jewelry, and property. With those documents and her testimony, you and your entire company will be destroyed and all of your stolen goods forfeited."

Julian grabbed the gun. "That was decades ago. If she has such information, why hasn't it surfaced? And where are those documents now?"

"In a very safe place, along with the diamonds. At first, she didn't know who she could trust or what she could do about it. Then, I have a feeling, she was trying to protect you. She knows you are up to your neck in the stink of your corporation, and she still loves you, but now she is doing the right thing."

"You don't know who you're dealing with, Mr. Stone. And when your fiancée gets here, I think you will have an attitude adjustment."

"If you hurt her, I will come after you."

"You don't scare me. You have no idea how deep the roots of our enterprise go."

"Then why don't you tell me?"

"No, I prefer that you tell *me* exactly where the documents and the diamonds are, if there are any documents."

"They're not in my house, so there's no use looking for them there. Your mother told me all about how your father came to their home and dragged the family away, your family. Are you following in your father's footsteps? Are you capable of murder?"

"I am very proud of my father and everything he accomplished. People today don't understand the importance of the Nazi movement and the significance of keeping Germany strong."

"Does keeping Germany strong require stealing from innocent people and selling their goods for profit? Taking over their houses like your father took over your mother's house, and trading on their misery? He certainly did not *purchase* it, as you say. I would expect something like that from your father, but you are also Hannah's child."

Julian spit at the floor. "My mother's name was Eva, and she never loved me or my father. Now I'm right where I belong, and I intend to get back what she stole from my father and from me. You'd be smart not to get in my way."

"Or what?"

"Believe me, you don't want to find out."

"You don't frighten me. And for the record, your mother did not have the diamonds all these years. I found them when I was renovating my home. I tried to give them back to her, but she wouldn't take them."

"Then she's a fool."

Julian made a call, and Herr Weber appeared.

"I have your ring, Mr. Stone." He handed over a velvet ring case to Alexander, who looked inside at the magnificent piece. It was polished to perfection and lit up the room.

"Hallelujah will love this." He placed the ring box on the table.

"Thank you, Otto," said Julian. "And now you will leave us. But kindly bring Fräulein Weiss back to us when she arrives."

The jeweler nodded and left the room.

"It's your choice, Mr. Stone. Take the ring and your fiancée and live your lives. You don't owe those people anything. Most of them are dead anyway, and they won't know the difference. They have no heirs. It's as if they never existed. So what if we want to make a profit? What's wrong with that?"

"What's wrong is that thousands of pieces of art were confiscated from the collections of Jewish citizens and were never returned to their rightful owners. Many of those pieces were stolen by your father and his friends, the profits of which you are now living on.

"And, on the contrary, those victims did exist and do exist. Abraham Hammerman and his first wife Madeline are very much alive, and so are their heirs," Alexander continued. "Mr. Hammerman has been trying to prove his ownership of several masterpieces that are currently hanging in museums around the world, and others are undoubtedly hidden away in private collections. Paintings that your father sold to them. We now have the paper trail to prove the provenance of those paintings, so if we can document Mr. Hammerman's ownership, these valuable paintings can be returned."

"There are numerous international organizations involved in restitution of stolen property during the war. What does that have to do with me? I wasn't even born then."

"Unfortunately, many of these organizations merely set up task forces that move at a snail's pace and do little or nothing to research provenance. So restoring possessions to the rightful owners could take years. That means survivors like the Hammermans must wait a lifetime for restitution and compensation, and they don't have a lifetime left to wait. With these documents and the deposition of Hannah Hirschfeld Grandcouer, your partnership will be linked with what your father called the U-Group. Luckily, they kept very precise records of who they stole from, exactly what they stole, and who they sold it to.

"And I imagine you've been sitting on some very valuable paintings in the decades since the war, anticipating higher profits in the millions of dollars. Perhaps the German Lost Art Database would be interested in those records. Perhaps you are hiding income. Who knows what they might find when your home and business are searched and your books examined? I imagine you don't always operate by the letter of the law. It's all about transparency, these days, or lack of it. I know the newspapers would love to break such a story. And the Israelis would love to get in on the action."

Julian picked up the weapon on the table, and his face was contorted with rage.

"You are in no position to threaten me." He leveled the gun at Alexander, and his hand shook as he tried to maintain a calm demeanor.

"I didn't want to have to do this. I am not a violent man. But you leave me no choice."

Alexander took a deep breath. This was not how he'd anticipated the day would turn out. He had fully expected to return home, propose to Hallelujah, this time properly, this time with a ring. Today was to be the beginning of their lives together. But sometimes it was a matter of right and wrong. And sometimes sacrifices had to be made.

"I don't care what you do to me. But please leave Hallelujah alone. She has done nothing. I was the one who got her involved in the first place. She knows nothing of the details of the documents."

Alexander noticed Julian's hand had ceased shaking. He must feel he was back in control. Better to keep him calm. He didn't relish getting shot.

"What is her life worth to you?"
"Anything. Everything."
"The diamonds?"
"Yes, you can have them."
"And the documents?"
"Those too."
"I need to know where they are. You will take me to them."

"What guarantees do I have, if I take you to them, that you will spare Hallelujah?"

Julian smiled. "You don't. You'll just have to trust me."

Alexander tried to think of a witty comeback, but reconsidered.

There was a knock on the door.

"It's me—Otto. They have the girl."

"Come in."

Two men entered the room with Hallelujah in their grip. When she saw Alexander she tried to run to him, but they restrained her. Her face twisted in pain.

"Don't hurt her, or you'll never find the diamonds."

"Let the girl go," Julian instructed his men. "That will be all for now, but keep watch outside."

Hallelujah ran to Alexander, and he kissed the top of her head and folded her in a bear hug. "It's okay now. You'll be okay."

"What is going on? These men came to the house and said they would take me to you, so I went with them, but then they put me in the trunk of their car."

Alexander tightened his grip on Hallelujah and stared accusingly at Julian. "Is that how you treat a lady?"

"If you cooperate, no harm will come to her. I assure you."

"What does he mean, cooperate? Who is he, Alexander?"

"This is Hannah's son by Herr Hoffman. I have something he wants—the diamonds and Hannah's documents—and if I turn them over, he says he will personally guarantee your safety."

"And you believe him?"

"No, but I don't see that we have any choice. I am going to take him to the diamonds."

Hallelujah looked up at the man with the gun. "But they don't belong to you."

"They were my father's property and now they're mine."

"They never belonged to you. Alexander, don't give them to him. And we need those documents."

Julian waved the gun. "This is getting tiresome. Herr Stone, we will go together to get the diamonds, and your lady friend will stay here with my security detail until we return. Any trouble, and I'll use this."

Alexander put his arm around Hallelujah's shoulder, took her face in his hands, kissed her lips, and said, "You wait here, and I'll be back before you know it." Then he turned to Julian.

"There's something I need to do first."

He picked up the ring box from the table, got down on his knees in front of Hallelujah and thrust it in front of Hallelujah.

"Is this—?"

"It's your engagement ring." He took the ring and placed it on her finger. "Will you marry me?"

She broke into a wide smile. "Yes, of course I'll

marry you. And I'll live with you anywhere." After all, these could be their last words. She didn't know if she would ever see him again.

"It's breathtaking. I love it and I love you."

"And I love you, Hallelujah." He placed the ring on her finger. "And now, it's official."

"Okay, enough sentimentality," snarled Julian. "It's time to go."

Alexander held Hallelujah as if he would never hold her again, and then kissed her softly. "This won't end here," he whispered. "I'll be back before you even miss me. I promise."

Hallelujah sat down on the chair Alexander had recently vacated and watched him walk out the door. Surely he realized he would be expendable after Julian got the diamonds and the evidence. They both were, and they'd both have to be disposed of.

Polly, I'm waiting for the cavalry, or at least Parker, to save us. Surely someone will come along and ride to the rescue.

When no one answered and nothing happened, Hallelujah sighed. She couldn't write her way out of this one.

What would Polly do in this situation?

Polly and Parker were as real to her as if they were flesh and blood. They'd been inside her brain for so long they were literally part of her. The actors who played the power couple had been together since the show started. There had been no "the role of Polly Winthrop is now being played by"—substitute name of revolving ingénue. Even when Polly woke up from a coma, her part was still being played by Shelley St. Clair. The role of Parker Sullivan had always been played by Russell Grainger.

Crap, it looks like it's up to me.

Frick and Frack, Julian's two kidnapping lackeys, were built like the Berlin Wall before the fall, but they were lacking in the brain department. Otherwise they wouldn't have left her alone in this dungeon, masquerading as a room. They'd snatched her so quickly that she still had her phone in her jacket pocket, and they hadn't tried to confiscate it. They'd grabbed her purse and assumed the cell phone, if she had one, would be in there. But they had no idea how connected she was to her cell. It was her lifeline. She hadn't used it until now because she thought she was being taken to Alexander, and that's exactly where she'd wanted to be. But now the situation looked grim. Hallelujah pulled out her cell phone and moved closer to the window. Could saving them be that simple?

She prayed her cell phone was charged and that she could get reception in this isolated backroom. But how did you call the police in Germany? 9-1-1? Zero for the operator? And would they speak English on the other end? And how did you say 'help' in German? Not to mention she had no idea where she was. Some jewelry store, probably in Dahlem. They hadn't driven far. Could they track her by her cell phone signal? And what would she say—"I've been kidnapped by two Nazis"? That ought to get their attention—if she could get through. Her fingers shook. What if the thugs came back before she could make the call?

And where had Julian taken Alexander? To his bank. But which one? There was a lot she didn't know about her future husband. A lot she still had to learn.

Think, Hallelujah. Remember the time Polly was

kidnapped by South American drug dealers and she had somehow untied herself and stolen their mobile phone to call Parker? What was the number she dialed? Hallelujah had researched it. The worldwide emergency number was 1-1-2. When you dialed 1-1-2, the network was supposed to automatically redirect your call to the local emergency dispatch. Would that number work in Berlin? Was 1-1-2 also the Pan-European emergency number? She couldn't be sure.

Here goes...

She dialed. What she heard on the other end was a steady stream of German she couldn't understand. *Great*, she had dialed the only emergency operator who couldn't speak English.

"Look, *Brunhilda*," Hallelujah said. "This is my life we're talking about." Hallelujah searched her brain, but the only German word she could come up with was *Auf Wiedersehen,* and it was certainly farewell if she couldn't connect with Hedwig, the one-language-wonder or Gretchen, the No-English-Spoken-Here *Fräulein.*

It was time to bring in the heavy guns.

"Polly Winthrop is in trouble!" she yelled. The voice on the other end suddenly grew excited, and she heard the operator parroting her words. "Polly Winthrop is in trouble. Polly Winthrop is in trouble."

She heard anxious voices in the background. Finally, some words she recognized. At least the agitated operator had the presence of mind to put her supervisor on the line.

"Mrs. Winthrop, can I help you? What is your emergency? Is it really you? Where's Parker?"

Hallelujah rolled her eyes. Action, at last.

Apparently, the Winthrop name opened doors around the world and could still work its magic.

"They've kidnapped Parker," Hallelujah sobbed, and then she rapidly explained her plight.

Chapter Twenty-Six
Alexander

Three Months Later

AS THE PLANET SPINS SCRIPT EXTRACT
BY HALLELUJAH WEISS
SCENE 7. THE BEDROOM OF THE WINTHROP ESTATE.
PARKER: I'm so proud of you, Pollyanna. You stayed calm in the face of danger. When you were kidnapped, I thought the worst.
POLLY: All I could think of was getting home to you, my darling. I was afraid I was never going to see you again.
PARKER: When the Coast Guard called and said you were safe, I actually broke down and cried. I'm never going to let you out of my sight again.
POLLY: Parker, I had faith in our love. We've survived a lot over the years. I wasn't going to let some South American drug lords come between us.
PARKER: We were destined to be together. I'll ask you again. Will you marry me?
POLLY: Yes, Parker. This time it's forever.

****

Alexander grabbed a copy of *The Berlin Daily Sun* from the newsstand and scanned the front page article that began above the fold. Everyone on the street was reading it. The banner headline was in 60-point type, usually reserved for funerals for heads of state, or the outbreak of war. But there it was, a complete exposé on *Zersetzung Gruppen KG,* with its spidery, Mafia-like ties to national German conglomerates, the government, including the police, and the sordid history of the enterprise. It referenced funds generated by stolen Nazi art and artifacts as the corporation's genesis during World War II, and the continued complicity of art dealers, auction houses, and museums around the world. There were lists of missing masterpieces, the names of the people they had initially belonged to, and the beginnings of the efforts to trace the original owners or their heirs.

After an intensive investigation, the profiteering officers of *Zersetzung Gruppen KG* had been hauled off to jail in handcuffs for fraud and graft. Julian Hoffman had tried to hide his face, but there was no mistaking him as the current head of the crime ring.

Hallelujah got more than her fifteen minutes of fame with the story about how the writer of the steamer *As the Planet Spins* had saved the day with her quick thinking, presence of mind, and a single phone call. Ratings for *As the Planet Spins* shot through the roof as Hallelujah gave all the credit to Polly. Hallelujah revealed that she had completed a novel mirroring the events in the lives of Hannah and Madeline.

But the real hero of the story was Hannah Hirschfeld Grandcoeur. Movie rights were being optioned for her story, with the working title, "The SS Sturmbannführer's Wife," amid much speculation about who would play the part of Hannah/Eva. Germany and the world still had a healthy appetite for anything Nazirelated. There was even a nostalgic, faded photograph in the paper of Franz Hoffman and his young, virginal bride, Eva, on their wedding day.

Hopefully, Hannah was back in Baden, blissfully unaware of the fervor surrounding the story that was breaking in newspapers across the globe, on network television, over the radio, and trending on social media. Alexander and Hallelujah had placed a private call to the facility in Baden, explaining to Hannah the progress they'd made.

And there were close-ups of the four stumble stones in front of Alexander's Dahlem house, documenting the grim statistics of the Hirschfeld family and the Holocaust. For a time, with the resurrection of collective German guilt, the number of anti-Semitic incidents, so rampant in the previous months, had plummeted.

This story had it all, like a good soap opera plot—love, desperation, betrayal, and finally—restitution. Hannah's sacrifice had paid off. Justice was served. All's well with the world. All was certainly well in Alexander and Hallelujah's world. The newlyweds had a meaningful ceremony at the *Neue* Synagogue on *Oranienburger Strasse* with Hallelujah's father Rabbi Weiss officiating.

Both sets of in-laws got along across the great German-Jewish divide with visions of grandchildren dancing in their heads. Hallelujah had confided that she had always wanted to start a family, but Lloyd was too busy to discuss it. Hallelujah crossed her hands discreetly at her waist and flashed an enigmatic Mona Lisa smile. They had decided her joyous news would stay secret from the world for a few more weeks.

And speaking of Lloyd and Livia, at the height of Hallelujah's popularity, Lloyd actually had the nerve to call and hint that he'd like Hallelujah back. It seems Olivia dumped Lloyd before their wedding when she caught him cheating on her with another woman. In the immortal words of the *rebbetzin*, "It couldn't have happened to a nicer couple."

Hallelujah finally got her trip to Italy. The couple honeymooned in Florence, and existed on a steady diet of pasta and love. Alexander promised himself to find out who Il Volo was, where in the world they were appearing at their next concert, and reserve tickets.

Which only goes to prove that your soulmate *can* literally fall out of the sky and that there *is* someone up there watching over us, orchestrating our happy endings.

Epilogue
Abraham Hammerman

The slender woman spinning across the stage was dark-skinned, with dark hair worn in a chic, chin-length bob and wide blue eyes. Greek or Italian, perhaps? The pull was palpable. It struck him like a punch in the gut and lower parts he thought were no longer working.

The lights were low. It could be an illusion. But it could also be her daughter. No, it would have to be her granddaughter. So many years had passed. The girl looked exactly like Madeline. Madeline had been a dancer. But that wasn't possible. His aging mind was playing tricks again. He'd often seen or thought he'd seen her riding on the *U-Bahn*, at an opera, just around the corner, on stage, certainly nightly in his dreams. He often had to remind himself that *his* Madeline was dead.

He had seen her red wool coat, the beautiful red coat he'd bought to keep her warm for their trip to America, lying in a pile of discarded clothes at the camp, outside the "showers" in the undressing area. He had inspected it. There was the couture label. It was an original. Madeline would never take off that coat, not if she were still alive. He couldn't save the love of his life. It was his biggest regret. His fingers traced the lining of the coat. The diamonds and American dollars she had sewn into it were still there. In the pocket he found their wedding picture, and he kissed it.

He fingered the red square of fabric in his tuxedo pocket like a talisman. He carried it with him everywhere. He'd even taken it to the ceremony when he married his second wife. When the war was over and he returned to his home, another family was living there. He had no proof that he had ever owned the home. The life he knew with Madeline was gone. He could never get it back.

But the darkness of the auditorium took him back. Back to a dark, smoke-filled room during an even darker time. His friend Julian Hirschfeld had gathered them at a hastily called meeting at his jewelry shop. They had all liquidated their assets—their jewelry, paintings, whatever they had of value, and given him all of their money. No contracts were needed, not between friends. And Julian was a lifelong friend. His wife, Ana, was Madeline's best friend.

Julian had produced a large velvet pouch and poured out the contents onto a black cloth. Flawless, fat, loose diamonds fell from his fingers like shooting stars in the heavens. Diamonds the likes of which he had never seen before. All beautifully crafted in the famous Hirschfeld style. The men in the room were stunned. They gasped, then held a collective breath. What they were looking at was priceless. What they were looking at would buy freedom for themselves and their families.

They were all given assurances that they would soon be in possession of the proper travel papers. They would leave the following week.

The music rose. The girl dancing on the stage looked so like his dead wife. The twist of her wrist, the curve of her neck, the texture of her hair, Madeline's hair. Tears pooled in Abraham Hammerman's eyes. Tears of love. Tears of regret.

"Mr. Hammerman, are you all right?" Alexander was seated next to his former boss and his bride, Hallelujah, was on Abraham's other side. They looked at each other in anticipation.

"It's nothing but an old man's mind wandering. It's just that that girl, the ballerina on stage, looks exactly like my dead wife Madeline. You know, my wife was a ballerina. We were so connected. I think I would know if she were no longer in this world, and she is still alive in my heart. I know that is impossible, but—"

The music rose again in a hopeful crescendo.

"Abraham—Mr. Hammerman, absolutely nothing is impossible," whispered Alexander. "We've arranged for a backstage pass after the show. There is someone—actually more than one someone—we want you to meet."

A word about the author...

Marilyn Baron writes humorous coming-of-*middle* age women's fiction, historical romantic thrillers, suspense, and paranormal/fantasy. A public relations consultant in Atlanta, she's a PAN member of Romance Writers of America (RWA) and Georgia Romance Writers (GRW) and winner of the GRW 2009 Chapter Service Award and writing awards in single title, suspense romance, paranormal/fantasy, and novel with strong romantic elements. She's also a member of the 2016 Roswell Reads Committee.

She graduated from the University of Florida in Gainesville, Florida, with a Bachelor of Science in Journalism (Public Relations sequence) and a minor in Creative Writing. Born in Miami, Florida, Marilyn lives in Roswell, GA, with her husband, and they have two daughters.

Marilyn Baron's Contest Wins

The Colonoscopy Club (now the published novel *STONES*) finaled in the GRW Unpublished Maggie Awards for Excellence in 2005 in the Single Title category.

The Edger won first place in the Suspense Romance category of the 2010 Ignite the Flame Contest, sponsored by the Central Ohio Fiction Writers chapter of RWA.

Sixth Sense won the GRW 2012 Unpublished Maggie Award for Excellence in the Paranormal/Fantasy Romance category.

Significant Others was a finalist in the 2014 GRW Published Maggie Awards for Excellence in the Novel With Strong Romantic Elements category.